No generative AI was utilized in the creative process, writing, editing, and publishing of this book.

Cover art by Blue Eyed Muse Art
Illustrations by Blue Eyed Muse Art
Edited by Twisted Thorn Editing House
Formatted by Feelin' Stabby Art

ISBN Paperback: 979-8-234-00753-7
ISBN eBook: 979-8-234-06108-9

The Stars in Our Hearts

STEVIE HOSLER

ILLUSTRATED BY
LAURA CANNELLA

DEAR WITCHES,

Your emotional well-being is my highest priority. The Stars in Our Hearts is a cozy fantasy, but it still explores serious issues that may be uncomfortable for some readers. This is perhaps the most personal book I will ever write, drawing from my own life experiences and trauma. While I promise you will laugh and experience joy, there may be some tears along the way, as these difficult but important themes are explored.

Domestic violence
Adultery
Femicide
Death of a Spouse
Parental Death
Political Violence
Misogyny
Patriarchal Systems of Oppression and Abuse
Homophobia (alluded to, but does not appear on page)

I hope you find comfort and light in Marcella and Chiara's story.

Additionally, this book is a period fantasy, not a historical fiction. While I have taken great care to accurately represent the names, clothing, turns of phrase, food, and culture of each time period, this is still, first and foremost, a fantasy book. I have taken liberty with historical events.

Take care of yourself,
Stevie

THE STARS IN OUR HEARTS PLAYLIST

We hope you love Taylor Swift.
Love, Stevie and Laura

1. Long Live- Taylor Swift
2. What it Sounds Like- HUNTR/X
3. Lavender Haze- Taylor Swift
4. But, What If I Fly?- Chrissy Costanza
5. You Set Me Free- Michelle Branch
6. Extraordinary Machine- Fiona Apple
7. Girl on Fire- Alicia Keys
8. Little Fires- Alanis Sophia
9. God is a Woman- Ariana Grande
10. Cosmic Love- Florence + The Machine
11. Rhiannon- Fleetwood Mac
12. Uninvited- Alanis Morissette
13. The Alchemy- Taylor Swift
14. The Smallest Man Who Ever Lived- Taylor Swift
15. Opalite- Taylor Swift
16. willow- Taylor Swift
17. dorothea- Taylor Swift
18. I Did Something Bad- Taylor Swift
19. peace- Taylor Swift
20. You're On Your Own, Kid- Taylor Swift
21. The Man- Taylor Swift
22. So Long, London- Taylor Swift
23. I Hate It Here- Taylor Swift
24. FLORIDA!!!- Taylor Swift, Florence + The Machine

For the women who found the missing piece of their heart in their best friend.

Let's create magic together.

ACT ONE

MONTEFIORALLE, ITALY

MAY 1582

SCENE ONE

MONTEFIORALLE

I HURRY INTO THE cottage, leaves trailing in from a gust of wind before I can shut the door against the brewing storm. "Whew! The gods are angry today." I tug the scarlet scarf from my head and shake out my soaked hair, dripping a puddle onto the stone floor of the four-room cottage I share with my best friend, Chiara Davazati.

"Quick, Marcella. Dry off by the fire before you catch your death," my friend calls to me from her place by the hearth.

My grandfather built this cottage and passed it to my father. I'm the third generation of Pallacioni to occupy our family home. The spirit of my departed family is nestled deep into the bones of every nook and cranny, from the kitchen where my mother lovingly prepared meals, the sitting area where we congregated to hear stories of my parents' youth, to the bedroom I shared with my younger sister, Paola. I still occupy the bed we shared. There is bittersweet comfort in remembering our late nights whispering secrets and fairy tales, buried beneath our blankets. The bed that once felt as large as a ship at sea somehow feels smaller without her.

Two summers ago, our families took ill when an incurable fever spread like wildfire through the village. The gods claimed our loved ones, leaving Chiara and me as the lone survivors of our bloodlines. We were fifteen then. I couldn't imagine living here without my family, but I also could not bring myself to leave.

Where would I go? I was not quite a child at fifteen years of age, but not yet a full-grown woman ready to marry and begin a family.

At my insistence that we could make it together, Chiara moved in, taking Mama and Papa's room and bringing with her the natural magic of her ancestors. Chiara's connection to flora and the earth's energy makes her a formidable botanist and apothecary. She speaks a language with nature that leaves me awestruck.

As a natural caretaker, I took up an apprenticeship with a midwife. The days are long, traveling to villages across the region to visit with women in need of my care. In the evenings, Chiara teaches me her craft, passing along her family tradition to me as her sister by choice and by fate. I have found I am empathic, finely attuned to the emotions of others.

My favorite pork stew is boiling over the hearth. The salty fragrance of fagioli e cotiche and the earthy, sweet yeast of freshly baked bread immediately warms me from the chill outside. I remove my muddy boots and stockings and hang my cloak on a peg near the door to dry before joining Chiara in the kitchen.

Herbs and flowers pinned in bunches to twine hang like garland from the rafters. Glass jars of salves, potions, and other remedies lovingly created by Chiara fill a cabinet against the eastern wall. Oils, beeswax, and tallow candles are strewn across the mantle above the hearth. Boards nailed into the wall next to the hearth hold jars of colorful preserves, honey, and vegetables, either from our garden or received as payment for our services.

My oldest friend stands at the well-loved worktable crafted by my father, hunched over her grimoire and grinding herbs with a mortar and pestle. I can see by the weariness on her face that she has been working tirelessly today as our village apothecary and alchemist. Flour covers her apron, and her fingers are stained a rose red from crushing flowers for candles she imbues with intention for her customers. Her strawberry-blonde hair is set in an intricate coronet that has come slightly undone throughout her work today, with a few stray wisps framing her face.

I set a bottle of wine in front of Chiara and kiss her cheek in greeting.

"From the De Gregani familia. A healthy bambina." I then retrieve a cloth bundle from my basket and hand it to her. "And this."

Setting down her work, Chiara wrinkles her freckled nose, looking in askance as she takes the cloth and carefully unwraps it. Her cerulean eyes twinkle, and she inhales the heavenly scent of ricotta and sugar from the flaky sfogliatella pastries. "Oh, Marcella. How were you able to afford this?" she breathes, worrying at her bottom lip.

We don't make much coin in our village. I help Chiara with the apothecary business, taking her potions and salves to sell or trade to my patients in my travels. We mostly deal in trade. A pastry this fine is a luxury we can rarely afford, but we make do and are never without the things we need most. Our neighbors take care of one another, ensuring there is food in every belly.

"A gift from Nonna De Gregani." I pull mismatched goblets from a shelf, pour the wine for our meal, and ladle stew into clay bowls while Chiara cleans her hands at the wash basin. Seated at our tiny table, we toast to the health of the De Gregani bambina and offer thanks to the All Mother, who breathes life into all living beings, for our meal.

Dipping a chunk of bread into her stew, Chiara asks about the birth.

"The birth was difficult for Guilia. The little one tore her, but I was able to staunch the bleeding and repair the damage. I left her one of your salves to help stave off infection and a few pouches of herbs for her to make into tea to alleviate the pain."

Chiara sits wide-eyed across from me. "And the baby?" Her heart is an endless well of love and kindness. I believe her potions and candles are powerful because her intentions are the purest of any person I've known. Her aura glows a soft, petal pink around her.

"A perfect little cherub. They call her Angela. But tell me about your day, you seem weary."

She sips her wine and sighs back into her chair. "I filled many orders for candles today. Everyone wants to guarantee a bountiful harvest and healthy livestock births this season. I feel like I bathed in poppy chamomile tea. And then Lorenzo came by— supposedly to trade for potions— but he didn't leave with anything after spending fifteen minutes chattering nonsensically and hovering like a spirit while I worked."

I can't help but smile at Chiara's annoyance with the lovestruck young man. Lorenzo has been trying to court Chiara for months, finding any excuse possible to visit our cottage. He comes from a good family. They own a farm just outside of town, raising livestock and tending an olive grove. His father bred my horse, and my work is only possible because he gave me a good deal in trade after my own family passed.

"Chiara, is your vision well?"

"Excuse me?"

I smile coyly at my opportunity to tease her. "You must be blind if you can't see that that boy is head over heels in love with you. Why don't you give him a chance?"

Her cheeks flush at the suggestion, and her hands fly up to cover them. "He is a *pest*!" she hisses. "That horrible hound of his relieved himself on my jasmine patch, and last week the beast went tearing through the garden chasing a squirrel and tore up my pepper seedlings! He is infuriating the way he just," she flicks a hand in the air, trying to come up with a word, "leers."

I burst out laughing. "He does not *leer*. The poor thing is so intimidated by you, his tongue twists into knots."

She huffs and crosses her arms. Her forehead crinkles, eyebrows knitted together in exasperation at my jests. "Well, I have no interest. It's not like I have a dowry to offer. Besides, I am perfectly happy here."

I know she is content in our life, but I want more for her, and I worry that if I don't push her, she will regret staying in this cottage with me. I could not bear her resentment. My work is my dream, my idea of the perfect life. It has always been my purpose, even before Death knocked on my door and carried away everyone in one fell swoop.

This life was not always Chiara's dream— to live in the village of our youth, barely scraping by and working our bodies to the bone just to ensure we have enough to fill our bellies. She wanted to spread her wings and fly, exploring the world with the love of her life, never staying in one place too long.

She is not meant for this pastoral life. She is the brightest star in the sky that the world has not yet met.

"Cara mia, my dear," I say gently. "You need not stay here for my sake. Dowry or not, you are special, and Lorenzo or any man would be blessed to have you. Think of the life you could have with his means! Think of your ability to travel as you always wished. He is well-off, kind, and handsome. I am only saying that you should consider the option."

Her expression softens, and the corners of her mouth turn down. "Do you not want me here?" Her voice is a breath of a whisper, and it makes my stomach drop. I reach across the table and take one of her hands in my own. They are soft despite the calluses from working in the garden and around the house. She has the hands of someone who does everything with care.

"Do not think that for a single second. You are my sister, and I love you. You can stay here forever, sail for faraway lands, or marry and stay in this village, and I will be happy just the same. I only worry that your kind heart keeps you here because you feel the need to be."

She squeezes my hand and meets my eyes, her gaze intense. "You are *not* an obligation, Marcella. My heart belongs here with you, dear sister. My heart lives in this cottage and in my magic. You are not my burden. You are my savior. I lost everything."

She pauses, and I feel the sharp sting of grief that comes when we speak of the families we lost not so long ago. Sometimes Chiara comes into my bed when the world is quiet, and we are left with nothing but the horrid visions of our families ravaged by sores and fever. We cling to each other, some nights crying ourselves to sleep, other nights sharing joy in the happier times with our siblings.

Chiara clears her throat and continues. "When you took me in, you opened my eyes to the possibility that I could spend my life practicing my craft and making a difference in the lives of others.

"I never believed I could use my magic to make a living and control my life's path. You gave me a gift." The glint in her eyes says more than her words ever could.

I refill our goblets and raise mine to her. "To sisterhood."

She raises her drink, and her face lights up brighter than the sun. "To sisterhood!" she proclaims gayly. We clink our goblets and drink.

We finish our meal and top off our wine, emptying the bottle, before retiring to our sitting room. Chiara speaks of expanding her business to other villages, traveling with me to sell her remedies, candles, and charms. The travel would allow her to find more regular customers.

Chiara talks of her dreams so openly. I've never heard her vocalize these new hopes for her future before. I suppose I always assumed she still wanted the life she dreamed of when we were children. Only now, I realize I've been so consumed by my own path that I missed when she flowered into her own person.

The person she has become is beautiful in spirit and stronger than I knew. But I still want to protect her as I always have. She is someone to be cherished for all that she is.

She is draped across a plush chair, feet dangling over the side, staring dreamily at the ceiling. "Do you think I'd make a good fairy godmother like in the storybooks? I can travel from place to place, granting girls wishes."

"Perhaps." I sip my wine. "But if it doesn't work out, you'd make a very fine bridge troll."

She scoffs at the notion. "And you would make an excellent evil queen."

I sigh heavily. "Chiara, I don't have a tower to lock you in. I would not be a successful evil queen."

Chiara hiccups and falls into a fit of giggles. A little piglet-like snort escapes her lips, and I join her in gales of laughter. Her cheeks and ears have a reddish hue, a clear indication that she has met her limit of wine for the evening. Her happiness is contagious, and selfishly, I am relieved that she has chosen to live this life together.

"Cara mia, you can do anything your heart desires. I promise, I will be here with you to see your dreams through."

She reaches her hand across the gap between our chairs and takes my hand. She swings our arms back and forth, absently, her brow furrowed in thought.

"Oh!" She drops my hand and stands suddenly, kicking her empty goblet across the floor, and rushes about the kitchen, pulling items from shelves.

Startled by her sudden burst of energy, I chase after her. "What has taken over you?"

She disappears under the worktable, riffling through baskets. "Ah!" She pops up triumphantly with a candle and bundles of dried flowers.

Clearing a spot on the worktable, she meticulously lays out her supplies. Curious and a little worried, I join her at the worktable, leaving dinner to be cleaned later. Clearly, Chiara has her heart set on something else at this moment.

I take inventory of everything on the table: a tallow candle that smells of freesia, matches, two small bottles of infused oils, a copper bowl, and bundles of dry lily of the valley and primrose. "Come!" she excitedly gestures for me to stand with her.

"What are we doing?"

"Patience, Marcella!" She situates the candle in the middle of the bowl, then arranges the flowers around the candle and pours the oils over them, murmuring an incantation of protection as she pours. When she is finished, she lights the candle and stands with her head bowed, eyes closed, hands hovering over the bowl.

I stand vigil, knowing she is spell-casting and it requires all of her attention. When she finally lifts her gaze, her eyes are clouded with tears, but a smile stretches from ear to ear. "Give me your hand. *Trust* me."

I trust her with my life, so I obey. Whatever she is planning, I know its purpose is to better our lives. She pricks my finger with a needle, and I yelp. "Chiara!" A bead of blood blooms on the tip. She does the same to her own, wincing at the pinch.

"Mi dispiace," she apologizes. She inhales deeply, then releases the breath slowly. "We are in this life together, Marcella. My heart belongs to you, mia cara sorella. What if we could *truly* be sisters? Would you commit your heart to mine, and mine to yours?" Chiara's crystal blue eyes glisten with hope as she bites on her lip, waiting for my response.

I am speechless. I miss Paola like a fish washed upon the shore would miss the sea. The All Mother blessed me with Chiara. She has helped heal the broken parts of me. Wiping at the tears threatening to spill down my face, I nod. "I would be honored to be your true sister, Chiara."

Exhaling a sigh of relief, she touches her fingertip to mine, mingling our blood so that we are now a part of one another. She holds her finger over the bowl and squeezes a few drops into it, then gestures for me to do the same. I force out a few drops before Chiara tips the candle to light the flowers, igniting them and filling our cottage with their ambrosial aroma.

We join hands, and she speaks, binding the spell.

"Sisters by choice,
Now sisters by blood.
Your heart is my heart,
Your soul is my soul.
May our souls become one,
And reunite upon our rebirth."

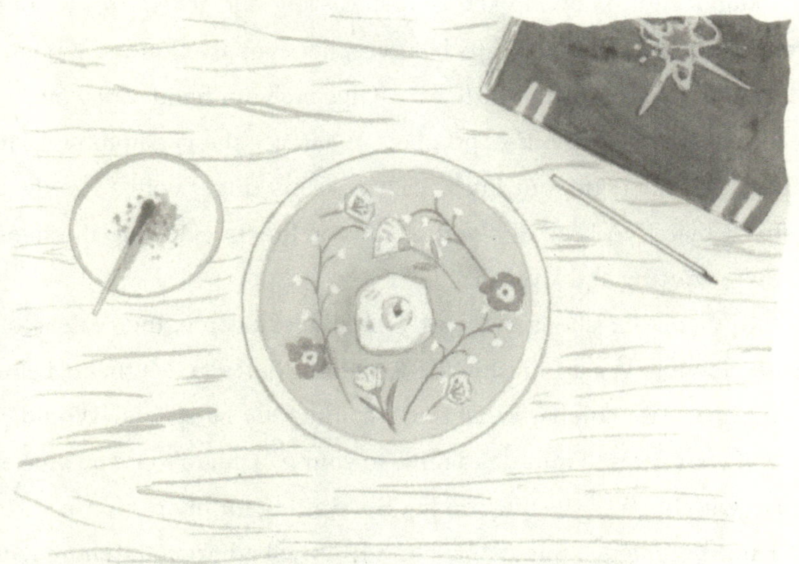

I repeat the spell with her. Tingles dance across my skin as it works its way deeper. It seeps into every fiber of my being, and I feel the moment a piece of me ceases to be. My breath catches at the sudden loss. The feeling is lonely. Cold. It is heartache and a cloud of melancholy. I hyperventilate, panicked by the well of emptiness carved from me.

I glance at Chiara, gripping her hand tightly. Her expression is pained, eyes desperate and focused solely on me, and I know she is experiencing the same loss.

The candle flares to life, the flame the color of cherry blossoms, illuminating our faces. And then it happens— the emptiness is replaced with something new. The hole within me stitches itself back together around the new piece.

Chiara's piece. I collapse against the table at the relief, still clutching her hand in my own. I pant, my heart racing. We stare at each other for a moment, utterly stunned, unsure of what to do or what to say.

Sweat drips down Chiara's temple from the exertion of casting the spell. And then she is on me, arms flung around my neck, her sweet laughter ringing in my ear. I hold her to me, my hands shaking. "We'll always be together, Marcella. Always."

I pull back, and that's when I notice the white halo of light surrounding us. Our auras have merged. Her pink glow and my green are replaced by a white light with gold flecks twinkling like fireflies on a summer night. It's the most breathtaking thing I've ever seen, and I'm overcome by its beauty.

It's us. Together.

I playfully flick my sister's freckled nose. "Always, Chiara."

"Always, Marcella."

SCENE TWO

MONTEFIORALLE

I AWAKEN THIS MORNING feeling full. Not from the food and decadent pastries from Nonna De Gregani, but full in a spiritual sense. I feel like... myself. More myself than I have been in two years. The gaping hole in my heart carved out by Death is no longer here. The ache and grief still stir within me, but somehow quieter. I place a hand over my heart, the steady thump thump thump beats against my hand. It's stronger, more persistent than it was yesterday.

It's Chiara. Our hearts beat as one in my chest, and I wonder if she is lying in her bed on the other side of the wall, noticing the same of her own heart. I don't hear her usual morning movement. She will need recovery time from the spell. It was the most powerful spell I've witnessed her cast, and it took quite a toll on her. I feel fatigued, my muscles ache slightly, but it is nothing I cannot push through.

Twilight is fading outside my window, the sky painted shades of lavender and thistle, and the stars blinking out for their daily slumber.

Today is a travel day. I have patients in another village to check in on. With a groan and an extra-long stretch, I begrudgingly pull myself from bed, intent to do some of Chiara's chores for her before I must leave so that she may rest.

I pull my nightdress over my head and notice a scar that wasn't here yesterday— a tiny star sits over my heart. I brush my fingers across it, and it tingles. Does Chiara have the same scar? It looks as though it has always been there, and it feels like it belongs. It is part of me.

I stare at it for another moment, feeling at peace with this new adornment, then dress in a green wool dress and set about my day.

After bringing the hearth to life and setting a pot of porridge to boil, I head outside to milk our goat and feed and brush my mare, Peony. Then, I visit the chicken coop to collect eggs while our hens scurry about the yard, feasting on the breakfast of stale crusts of bread and grain I scattered for them.

The dawn air still has a late-spring chill, and unfortunately, my boots are soggy once more from the damp earth beneath my feet in the wake of last night's rains. When I return to the cottage, I set them by the fire to dry and hope that it will be enough before I depart.

A door creaks and Chiara emerges from her room, bleary-eyed, hair a mess of tangled waves from unwinding her coronet. She holds a floral shawl tightly around her and hurries to sit by the hearth to soak up its heat. She looks exhausted.

The kettle whistles, announcing it is ready, and I pull it from the hearth, preparing us tea with mint and honey. She notices the eggs and pail of milk and fixes me with a glare. "Marcella, why are you performing my chores?"

I ignore her frustrated tone. "You need rest, cara mia. I can pick up some extra work for the day. Think nothing of it." I hand her the cup of tea and fill our bowls with porridge, adding a bit of nutmeg and honey. She is holding her clay cup with both hands, warming herself. "Come." She stands from her stool to join me at the table for breakfast. "*Mangia*. Eat. You need to regain your strength."

She takes a large bite of porridge, making a show of swallowing and shoveling in another bite. Even in her display of indignation, there is playfulness in her movements. "Happy?"

I sip my tea, acting nonchalant, knowing it will pick at her nerves. "Keep eating, cara mia." I grin deviously over the rim of my cup.

"Oh, for the All Mother's sake." Her spoon clatters on the table, and I bite back a laugh while she rubs her fingers to her temples. "It is too early for your teasing. I'm putting something in your wine tonight to make you sleep through tomorrow morning so I may know a moment's peace."

"I expect nothing less. You are diabolical." My heart pounds more firmly, and I know I've rattled her enough for one morning. I rub at my chest and remember the scar. "I have a new scar. It's over my heart." I pull my dress down to show off the star. "Is it from the spell?"

Chiara looks down at her nightdress. "I have one, too. It must be where our soul fragments traveled between our bodies." She smiles to herself, examining it. "It's quite adorable. Piccola stella." Little star.

I shake my head and chuckle, then tuck into my own porridge. No sooner is the spoon to my mouth when there is a knock at the door.

I glance up from my bowl. Chiara's face is scrunched in confusion. "Who in the world can that be at this hour? The sun is barely up." She pulls her shawl across her body, attempting modesty as she is still in her nightdress, and pads the short distance to the door and cracks it open. "Bonjourno. May I help you, signori?"

Signori? I abandon my breakfast and hurry to the door, nudging Chiara aside. "Get dressed. I will attend to our visitor." I smooth out my skirts and step outside. Four older gentlemen are crowded around my stoop. I recognize one as Padre Antonio, the priest from our village, but the other three are unfamiliar to me. I am overcome with unease, but I stand straight and keep my voice pleasant.

"Bonjourno, signori. How may I help you this morning?"

"We wish to speak with the patriarch of the house," the one immediately before me demands. His features are hard, eyes cold and devoid of emotion. His graying hair is thinning on top, and wisps blow erratically in the light breeze.

I affix a bright smile to my face that makes my cheeks ache from the force. "Well, that would be me, I suppose. This is my family home, and I am the sole member of my family." His brown eyes grow wide, and he looks down at me like I am an insect swimming in his soup. "So, as Chiara has asked, how may we help you?" This time, I drop all pleasantries from my voice. I will not be intimidated by a man on my own property.

Padre Antonio pushes his way to stand next to this crude man, and for a brief moment, I am grateful for his presence. He has been our town's preacher since before I was born and baptized both Paola and me. "Marcella Pallacioni, you and Chiara Davazati have lived in sin for two years. You stand accused of practicing witchcraft, summoning the will of the Devil, and committing lewd acts against the grace of God."

I choke on a laugh. "Surely you jest. Padre Antonio, you have known Chiara and me since we were but babes running through the village. It is not a crime for two orphaned young women to live together so that they may survive. Are we not contributing members of this community? Do we not provide services to the health of our neighbors?"

"The way you live is improper and against God. We know what happens in this cottage. We know the impure trinkets and potions you peddle about the village and surrounding towns. We know the sinful, carnal nature of your relationship."

Rage fills me, and my blood heats, heart racing like a rabbit fleeing a wolf. Chiara must feel my anger mirrored in her own chest. She attempts to push her way out of the house, but I quickly shut the door behind me, blocking her only exit.

I prop my hands on the ample swell of my hips and sneer at the man who spoke first. "On what authority do *you*, signore, come to *my* home and accuse me of such misdeeds? What proof have you brought?"

"Signorina Pallacioni, I am Lucido Albizzi, Inquisitor of Firenze. I am here in response to the good Father's missive." His lips curl in a cruel, heinous smile. It's the smile of a demon descended from the very bowels of Hell. "You will do well to remember your place, signorina, in the presence of a man of God and officials here on government business."

My stomach twists at his veiled threat. There is a dark undercurrent to his words, his tone, his entire demeanor. I nod once in understanding, but hold firm to my place in front of the door. I sense Chiara's presence on the other side, listening intently.

"Now then, step aside. We are to inspect the premises. If we find nothing of consequence, we will leave you in peace with my full apology for disturbing the ladies of the house, and we can put this ugly business behind us." Inquisitor Albizzi's eyes burn with malice.

My mind flashes to Chiara's grimoire, and I try to keep my expression placid, giving away none of the trepidation I feel building in my chest. I hope Chiara has heard and is stowing away the book that details generations of family spells, potions, and botany. I nod again, slowly, trying to delay their entry for even a second more.

I turn and lead the Inquisitors and Padre Antonio into our cottage, and I immediately feel the violation of it all. The tranquility of our home shifts to an air of hostility. These men corrupt the sanctuary that my cottage has always been for me. I hold in the sigh of relief nestled in my chest when I see Chiara has changed into a simple dress and apron. Her hair is pinned back in a loose twist, and she is seated at the table, drinking her tea.

She smiles warmly at the intruders but does not move from her seat. "Signori. May I offer you some tea to warm you on this chilly morning?"

The Inquisitor looks down his nose, assessing her. "No." He holds two fingers up to his companions. "Benedicto, Ilio. Search the property." He never breaks eye contact with Chiara, and she, likewise, does not back down.

Our home devolves into chaos. They tear into our belongings with reckless abandon. Potions are confiscated into satchels, and baskets of flowers and herbs are emptied onto the floor. Chiara leaps from her seat, and I rush to hold her in place before she does something regrettable. I can feel her distress, her fear, her anguish.

I hold her to me and say into her ear so only she can hear, "Be calm, cara mia. This storm shall pass. We'll set it right."

I say the words, but I do not feel the truth in them. Our kitchen is in shambles. One of the inquisitors is uncorking bottles, smelling the remedies I use with my patients. The other flings open the door to my bedroom, and I see red. I release Chiara and rush across the cottage, careful not to step on our belongings that are now so carelessly strewn across the floor, already trampled by their feet.

"Signore! What business have you in a woman's bedroom?" He is digging through the chest of drawers, his disgusting hands fisting my under garments and nightdresses as he looks for the All Mother knows what. "This is improper and a violation of my privacy." He ignores me, and I try to pull him from my room, grasping at the garment in his hand. He flings his arm out, knocking me off balance. I trip backwards over the corner of my bed and land hard on the floor, sending pain radiating through my bottom and up my spine.

My blood boils. "Arrrgh!" I pull myself to my feet and lash out at him, raking my nails across his face so hard that I draw blood.

"Benedicto! Seize this woman," he calls out to the other man, who is currently tearing through a cabinet just outside of my bedroom door. "She is hysterical. There is something here she does not want us to find."

My world tilts as large arms consume me, lifting me and carrying me from my room. I thrash like a wild animal, kicking and demanding that he release me. I'm back in the kitchen, surrounded by the shards of my broken life. Padre Antonio is at the center of it all, the picture of calm: the eye of the storm. Inquisitor Albizzi is nowhere to be seen, but Chiara's bedroom door is open. My eyes frantically scan the cottage for my sister. I hear her cries from her bedroom and the sharp *crack* of skin assaulting skin.

A guttural growl rips from me, scratching my throat. "Take your hands off of me!" I stomp on my captor's foot, but he holds firm, squeezing me tighter until it is difficult to breathe.

Inquisitor Albizzi sweeps out of the bedroom, dragging Chiara by her hair. He flings her to the ground as though she were a rodent he found in his kitchen. She lands with a hard thud and curls in on herself, bracing herself for another blow that does not come. "Signori!" The man in my bedroom reappears, red-faced and breathing heavily from exertion from tearing my home apart. I feel satisfaction at the long, bleeding scratches marring his hideous face.

Benedicto turns me to face the Inquisitor. Padre Antonio glances my way, and for a moment, I see something flash in his eyes. He looks... triumphant.

"Padre Antonio, I have found irrefutable evidence that these women are engaged in dark magic." He raises the grimoire in the air, victorious. My stomach plummets. Chiara pushes herself up and looks to me, crestfallen. Her lip is split, stained crimson, and the side of her face is swollen. His handprint is a brand upon her cheek. Her hair is wild and undone, dress askew and torn. I can feel her despair within me. I feel her sorrow. She feels responsible. I shake my head at her and try with all my might to send a message from my heart to her own that she did nothing wrong.

My sister hangs her head, tears falling silently, body trembling ever so slightly. She's trying to be strong, but it's no use. I feel the same defeat as her, and I am overcome by fear of what they will do to us.

Padre Antonio crosses the room to the Inquisitor and plucks the grimoire from his hand. He studies the pages, face neutral.

I'm desperate. I cannot allow these men to determine our fate. "Padre, per favore. It is just a book of remedies. Cures for headaches, salves for injuries. It is medicine. Science." I try to keep my voice steady and calm. Confident.

He turns a page, paying me no mind. Benedicto shakes me and growls in my ear, "Silenzio, strega."

Witch.

Minutes tick by. The only sounds that fill our cottage, usually vibrant with laughter, are the sharp turning of pages, Chiara's hitched breaths from her weeping, and Benedicto's breath in my ear. He smells of tobacco, sweat, and goats. I turn my head from his disgusting mouth. My skin itches from his unwelcome touch.

Finally, Padre closes the book and tosses it into the hearth. Chiara picks herself up and rushes to the fire, wailing as the book passed down through generations withers and burns, killing the last remaining thread of her family.

I feel the moment her heart splinters, sending pain radiating through my chest. It shudders through me like earth tremors.

Inquisitor Albizzi's voice booms through our fractured home. "Marcella Pallacioni and Chiara Davazati, you have been found guilty of witchcraft. By the will of our Lord, you shall be punished for your crimes at sundown. Benedicto, Ilio. Bring the girls to the stockade."

They force us from our home, dragging us through the doorway into the spring morning. It is startling, the contrast of the beauty and life blooming around us as our lives are in ruins. Chiara is fighting Ilio tooth and nail, raging against his hold. I don't fight. It's what they want from me, and I will not give them the satisfaction of seeing me break again.

The Inquisitor pauses at the garden gate. He turns ever so slowly, drawing out the moment of whatever horror he is about to commit. "Cleanse this house of the evil that dwells here. Burn it."

And with those words, I shatter.

SCENE THREE

MONTEFIORALLE

WE'RE TAKEN TO THE village square, tied to posts, and left there for hours. I am parched, and my skin is inflamed from the sun beating down upon me all day without the protection of shade. Our neighbors hurry by, murmuring behind their hands. Chiara has no tears left to cry and leans slack against her post, staring at the ground before her.

Me? I am fury embodied. I let it simmer, staring at these people who have known me my entire life as they gossip and treat us as a spectacle.

I am no spectacle. I will not be their entertainment.

And yet, despite it all, my mind can't help but think of the happy memories I have accumulated here over my short life. Trips to the market with Mama. Papa seated behind me on our horse, letting me hold the reins and making me feel so grown. Whispering secrets about boys with Paola while we ate sweets on our way home from our lessons. Dancing at weddings in the square— Chiara, Paola, and I swinging each other around in our best dresses until we lost our balance and fell to the ground together.

I let those memories wash over me, let them bolster my strength as we await our sentencing.

I look to my sister. She is despondent. The blue of her eyes has gone gray with worry. "*Cara mia.*" She doesn't respond. "Chiara, per favore. Look at me." She doesn't move her body, but her eyes glance my way. "No matter what happens, I am with you. I am with you, and I am a part of you. You are a part of me. They cannot take that from us."

I barely hear her voice. "Mi dispiace, Marcella. I'm sorry, my sister."

"There is nothing to be sorry for. They destroyed our peace. Not you. *You* are my peace."

"And you are mine."

A tear slips free from my eye. My hands are bound behind me, wrists sliced through and bleeding from the ropes. The scar on my chest is pulsating, and I long to touch it. To feel my sister's heart beating against my own hand— to know that together, we are complete.

The light of day is fading fast. I hear her teeth chattering with the chill as the sun disappears over the horizon. We have no cloaks to protect us from the cold.

The chapel's bells toll, foreboding and ominous, striking out the time with seven chimes. It is as though the musical quality of the bells has been replaced with oppressive melancholy.

A crowd is gathering, beckoned by the sound. Padre Antonio and Inquisitor Albizzi lead a procession of the congregation out of the chapel and into the square. His disciples surround Chiara and me, glowering at us with disdain. I look around at the crowd of familiar faces: the neighbors I have healed, the babies I have birthed into this world, the people I have known since I was just a child myself.

Padre and the Inquisitor remain on the chapel stairs. Chiara and I face them from our positions in the square. Padre holds his arms out in a gesture of silence, then steps forward. "Today, we gather in the face of evil. Even in a village such as this, where we love our neighbors and live in the image of our savior, Lord Jesus Christ, we are not immune to the allure of darkness. We are not immune to the seductive promises of power from the fallen angel Samael."

Padre Antonio descends the stairs, stepping forward until he is standing just out of reach. He catches my eye and turns his nose up at me before returning his attention to the crowd.

"These women, Chiara Davazati and Marcella Pallacioni, have turned their backs on the light and goodness of God. They are corrupted by Samael, living in sin and thrusting their evil upon the good disciples of this community. They claim to be but humble healers, but their deception has been uncovered, and we bring them before us today to serve as an example of God's judgment."

Inquisitor Albizzi joins Padre Antonio before us. I raise my head and stare him down in challenge. He will not intimidate me. "We thank the good Padre for his vigilance in the face of corruption. These are dangerous times. But there is a lesson to be learned. Evil wears many masks. These women are proof that the devil is among us. For their crimes and in protection of our village, I hereby sentence them to death by burning."

The crowd erupts, but I do not hear them. All I hear is the beating of my own heart in my ears. Something hits me in the face, and the world comes back into focus. Our neighbors are in a frenzy, throwing anything available to them at us. Benedicto and Ilio begin setting up the pyre around us, piling wood and hay.

Chiara's cries reverberate through my body. The brilliance of our shared aura has dulled and hangs over us like a shadow.

I don't know what to do. I don't know how to save us.

Chiara is begging for mercy. "Will no one stop this? Signora Nobili. You know what these men speak is not the truth. You know me. You knew my family. Will you not speak on our behalf?"

The elderly woman turns away from us. Others do the same. Do they believe that if they do not look upon us, they are not culpable for our deaths? Our blood will stain the hands of every person here, whether they believe it or not.

I cannot contain my fury any longer. "You are cowards. All of you! How dare you judge us while you stand by, gleeful to watch us burn. We who have protected you and healed you when you needed us most. Cowards!"

I scream my throat raw, throwing accusations at our neighbors. They continue to bombard us with food and stones, and my rage only grows as I continue to curse them for the hypocrites they are.

Our neighbors were all too happy to accept our services when it benefited them. But now? As we stand accused of evil, they refuse to implicate themselves. Their souls will be damned for their cowardice.

I do not flinch as a stone catches me above my eye, and I feel my blood, warm and thick, trickle down the side of my face. But Chiara… my beautiful sister is overcome with fear. Raging against her bonds, she howls with desperation for a savior to show themselves among the riot before us.

"Marcella! Marcella, what do we do?" Her eyes are bloodshot, her voice hoarse from hours of crying. I can scarcely hear her over the violent roar of the crowd, chanting, "Bruciare le streghe!"

Burn the witches.

I don't know how to save us.

The crowd parts before us, making way for Inquisitor Albizzi. He bears a torch: a flame to snuff out our light. It's ironic.

Sneering at us down his nose, he grants us one last right. "Do you have any last words?"

I spit in his face. It's my final act of defiance. I will not give him the satisfaction or the gift of my thoughts. Without a word, without even wiping my saliva that drips down his wretched face, he tosses the torch at my feet. My skirts immediately catch. My sister is hysterical beside me, the fire spreading to her in an instant.

"Chiara. Look at me, sorella." The heat is unbearable as it licks at my skin, threatening to swallow me whole. Through the blinding smoke, I catch her eye one final time, using her to gain enough strength to force out my final words around the pain surging throughout my body— my final goodbye. "Ti amo, Chiara. I love you. I will find you."

"Ti amo, Marcella. Always."

The fire roars around us. I can't breathe. The smoke chokes me. It's so loud. Consuming.

The last thing I see is a burst of white and gold.

It's so beautiful.

It's so-

ACT TWO

LONDON, ENGLAND

JULY 1682

SCENE ONE

LONDON

MY HANDS ARE SMUDGED black with ink. Stretching my fingers to alleviate the cramp from hours of writing, I inhale the rich fragrance of roast chicken and herbs wafting through the manor. My husband, the Lord Charles Jameson, is expected home for supper soon, no doubt.

I have been stowed away in the drawing room since just after lunch, drafting a story. Charles thinks little of my passion. He believes my time is better spent on other crafts more befitting the wife of an attorney. Needlepoint and the pianoforte bring me little joy, and my ability to paint is dreadful. These tedious hobbies are much more for his amusement than my own. Burying my nose in a book or drafting tales of my own is an "undignified way" for Lady Audrey Jameson to occupy her time— or so he claims.

Charles has assembled quite an enviable library, though he prefers I do not disturb his study. It is just as well, as his collection does little to thrill me. Essays and histories are a bore. I long for adventure. I wish to lose myself in the pages of a faraway land, to read of love so passionate that it makes my heart burst with excitement and brings tears to my eyes.

No. Charles' library does not have what my heart desires. Most libraries and bookshops do not. And so, I have taken it upon myself to create that which I do not possess. The stories in my mind and in my heart now exist on the rolls of parchment stowed in the pianoforte bench. I head to the wash basin and try with all my might to scrub the ink from my fingers, erasing evidence of my day.

When Charles arrives home, I am seated upon my stories, halfheartedly practicing scales.

Our marriage was not a love match. I consider myself a business deal, for Charles began his career clerking for my father, making me a mere consolation prize for a partnership at Father's firm. Charles comes from the noble House of Jameson. We're happy enough, I suppose. We get along most days, so long as I mind myself in a manner befitting the "Lady of the Manor." It is an impossible feat, truly, as I do not possess the countenance nor the temperament of Charles' vision of a lady.

I have long suspected he keeps mistresses, but I haven't the heart to care. These women do me a great service, leaving my evenings to myself. I can exist in peace, reading the precious few romance novels I keep hidden away in my wardrobe and pouring my energy into my writing.

I know I am a disappointment. I am odd, a daydreamer. Some days I feel as though I were born into the wrong body or the wrong life. I've felt this way since I was a young girl. My Lady Mother and governess tried to mold me into a perfect, mealy-mouthed little debutante, but I could not be tamed. I spent my time with torn dresses and dirt under my nails from playing in the meadows and tree groves on our estate.

Despite my best efforts, I still find myself confined to tight bodices and balls far too often, prattling on about nonsensical gossip among the other noble wives. I am bound by the shackles of man. To my father and my husband, I am nothing more than a transaction, and it is stifling.

Charles approaches and places a chaste kiss upon my cheek. "Good evening, Audrey. You look lovely today." His tone is clipped, posture rigid. I cannot discern if his compliment is genuine or simply a polite obligation. I had visited the modiste the day before to pick up the new dresses I ordered. The pale blue fabric and beadwork of my dress make my brown eyes stand out in contrast, and the bodice accentuates my generous curves.

"Thank you. The modiste did a most remarkable job."

He removes his jacket and hovers as I tinkle away at the keys, no doubt waiting for me to provide some source of entertainment. I transition to a simple song, but fumble several times. Charles scowls at my noticeable mistakes. "I'll send for a proper instructor in the morning. I must attend to some correspondence in my study. I will join you for supper within the hour."

I nod, forcing a demure smile. His gaze lingers a moment longer, dropping to my hands, causing his eyes to narrow. I quickly tuck them into my skirts. I know he sees the ink dried upon my fingers. My hands are so thoroughly stained that I am no longer able to fully cleanse myself. The ink is a part of me.

I brace myself for sharp words, but none come. He straightens himself and quits the room, walking stiffly, feet heavy upon the wooden floorboards.

I allow myself to breathe, thankful to have avoided his scorn. If only my hands were dyed pinks and yellows with paint, my husband might fancy me a proper wife— a wife worthy of his pride.

Dinner is a quiet affair, as it is most evenings. The dining room echoes only with the clinking and scraping of the silverware against our plates. Charles excuses himself for the evening, saying he is meeting colleagues at the gentlemen's club.

I retire to my bedroom, hoping Charles will tire himself out with whomever he is truly meeting and leave me be when he arrives home smelling of tobacco, whiskey, and the floral scent of his lover's perfume.

My lady maid Lucy helps me out of my dress and unwinds the pins from my hair, letting my brown locks fall in soft curls around my shoulders. I quickly plait it and settle into my bed while she bustles about, tossing another log on the fire and ensuring that everything is in order before she herself retires to her quarters for the evening. I thank her for her help, and she quietly curtsies and leaves me.

Once I hear her footsteps disappear down the hall, I leave my bed and dig through my wardrobe to the back and pull out a hatbox. I carefully select a book about a knight and his love affair with a girl from a peasant village. It's scandalous, but I cannot help but envy the girl for her ability to choose love.

After a few chapters, my eyes grow heavy with sleep. I tuck the book under my pillow and blow out the candle in my bedside lantern. I drift to sleep with thoughts of being swept away from this place on my mind.

SCENE TWO

LONDON

IT'S PLEASANT WEATHER TODAY. It would do me good to be out of the drawing room, and I do fancy a trip into town. I have need of more parchment, and I should like to visit the patisserie. An afternoon writing and stuffing myself with cinnamon tarts sounds more appealing than pianoforte lessons.

The book I read last night has inspired me. Why should I not write of the love I desire? There must be other women who ache as I do to be wild and carefree. I cannot be the only woman who yearns for passion.

On my walk home from the patisserie, I pass by a new storefront and immediately stop to admire the paintings on display in the window. I am so compelled that I feel my hand reaching almost involuntarily for the door. I step inside the shop, balancing my package of tarts and rolls of parchment. Dozens of paintings hang on the walls and stand on easels. I take my time moving about the room, admiring the detail of each masterpiece.

The architecture and pastoral landscapes are breathtaking. Vivid. Rolling hills and greenery somehow subdue the castles, as though the artist is painting in quiet rebellion of nobility. I long to visit the places that inspired such beauty.

The melodic greeting of a woman wrenches me from my daydream. "Bonjour, madame." I nearly jump free of my skin. My parchment falls to the floor, but I manage to hold tight to my cinnamon tarts. "Je suis désolé, madame. I did not mean to give you a fright." She bends to collect my items and hands them back to me. Her English is perfectly enunciated, layered with the elegant roll of her French accent.

She seems strangely familiar. She is tall and lithe, with golden hair tucked into a loose bun and freckles scattered across her nose like stars. She wears a simple dress and an apron stained a kaleidoscope of colors. There is a bit of red paint smeared across her brow. I smile to myself as it reminds me of the ink still staining my own hands.

I tilt my head and try not to stare at her, but there is something there that I cannot place my finger on. "I am called Georgette Marchand." She offers her hand, and I take it. She dips into a quick curtsey.

"Audrey Jameson. Pleasure to meet you."

"You as well, my lady. I see you have an eye for this painting," she says, nodding at the landscape before me.

My attention is returned to the piece. "Yes," I say, enamored with the color. "It's brilliant. Are you the artist?"

"I am a merchant for the artist Jean Rousseau Bonnet of Le Mans. His art is most coveted in Paris."

"Oh, apologies, Miss Marchand. You are covered with paint! I assumed you were the artist."

She offers me a kind smile, but her nose wrinkles ever so slightly. "Can you imagine? A woman selling her art in a gallery? Do we dare dream?" She lightly bumps her shoulder against mine and gives a mischievous wink.

I immediately know that I like Georgette. I haven't any friends. Perhaps this meeting today was fortuitous. "How much for the painting?"

"One hundred guineas, my lady. However, I think for a woman such as you who appreciates the arts, we could part with it for ninety?" I notice her gaze has slid to my ink-ridden hands.

"I'll send my husband's butler to fetch it this afternoon, but I will pay full price. An artist should know their worth and be compensated fairly." I deliberately hold her stare for an extra moment. "And please, call me

Audrey."

Her lip quirks up slightly, and that impish light in her eyes comes alive. She nods and bows. "As you wish. I will wrap it up. And you must call me Georgette." She collects the painting and takes it to the back room. I continue sauntering about, my stomach complaining that it is almost time for lunch. Georgette reappears, and I settle the matter of payment.

As I head for the door, something in my chest tugs at me. I halt, my hand on the knob. "Georgette, I'd like very much for you to join me for lunch."

She looks surprised. She's absently rubbing at a spot on her chest. "Oh. I am not certain I am dressed for a lunch outing." She pulls back her apron to show more paint splashed upon her skirts.

"Oh, nonsense. You'll join me in my home for lunch and tea. It is just a few blocks walk."

"I don't wish to impose."

"It's no imposition. Consider it a favor. I'd love to have someone to speak with who is concerned with matters other than petty neighborhood gossip about who's husbands are fornicating with their governesses and secretaries."

Georgette nearly chokes on a laugh. I hold my hand out to her. "Shall we?" She retrieves the store keys from behind the counter and rushes to the door.

SCENE THREE

LONDON

LUNCH WITH GEORGETTE WAS a breath of fresh air. It made me realize how lonely I am in this house by myself. She is delightful company. Sharp-witted and ostentatious. Georgette carries herself as though she has a secret, and she wants everyone to know she is keeping one but will not share.

But I know her secret. It is obvious if one simply pays attention.

However, most people do not give a woman a second glance or believe us to be clever.

Robert, Charles's butler, escorted her back to the store in our carriage to retrieve the painting. I think I will hang it in the drawing room. The artwork in this room is dour, and I do not care for it. If I must spend my days wasting away in this room, then I should at least have something pleasing and cheerful to look upon.

Something that *I* selected.

I am examining the room for the perfect place to display my painting when I hear a knock at the door. Lucy's footsteps clack across the foyer. A few moments later, she joins me in the drawing room. "My lady, a messenger just delivered this for you." She hands me a folded piece of parchment.

My dearest, Audrey,

I must attend to an important business matter and will not return until late this evening. My deepest apologies for leaving you for a second night this week. I shall see you in the morning to break our fast.

Yours, Charles.

I suck my tongue against my teeth and fold the note. "Thank you, Lucy. My lord husband shall not be home for supper."

"Yes, my lady." She turns to return to her chores, and I call her back. "Lucy, a moment please." I pull a piece of stationery from the desk and hastily scribble a note. "When Robert returns, please have him deliver this back to the art gallery. I will take my dinner on the terrace this evening. For two. Please let the kitchen know that I will have a guest." She takes the note, curtsies, and hurries from the room.

I stand back from the fireplace with my hands bracing my lower back and stare at the painting of a man on horseback. The color is drab, his expression severe. "I think it is time we make some changes in the Jameson household."

A few hours later, my new painting is hanging above the fire in the drawing room, and I sit on the terrace sipping a glass of wine, quite satisfied with myself. The July evening is warm, and the air is rich with honeysuckle. The patio door opens, and Lucy escorts Georgette outdoors. "Miss Marchand is here for your visit. I will return shortly with your supper."

"Thank you, Lucy. Please bring Miss Marchand a glass of wine as well."

"Yes, of course, my lady." She curtsies and disappears back into the house.

Georgette greets me, placing kisses on each of my cheeks. "Audrey, your garden. C'est beau." She wanders about the terrace, running her fingers along the boxes of flowers.

"I am glad the evening is so warm that we can take our meal out of doors. Would you like a tour of the gardens?"

"Oui, merci." I lead her through the gardens. Frogs croak and hop about the pond, and Georgette laughs. "Audrey, this is a fairytale." Weeping willows sway along the pond's perimeter, and white roses and ivy climb the stone wall enclosing the gardens. "I would spend all of my days out here."

"I spend as much time as I can when the weather permits. But there are my duties as Lady of the house that I must attend to, and it can keep me trapped in the drawing room some days. I will not bore you with the details." How I long to spend my days outdoors, writing on the patio or lazing about under a tree with my nose in a book. I grimace at the thought of the pianoforte lessons that will no doubt begin within the week.

We begin our walk back to the patio. Lucy should arrive any moment with our meal. "Your garden is beautiful enough to paint. It's inspiring, truly."

Pride rises in my chest at the compliment from someone such as Georgette, who obviously has a keen eye for beauty. "You are welcome to paint the grounds any time you wish."

Georgette's eyes light up. "Do you mean it?"

"On the condition that we have tea and cakes together before you start."

"You are quite the shrewd negotiator, Audrey. I accept your offer." We sit at a small table, and Lucy brings a tray, setting our plates and Georgette's wine before us. Our plates are piled with roast duck in gravy, summer vegetables, and hearty bread with butter.

The tug in my chest returns, and once more, I notice Georgette fussing about her own chest. She touches the same spot where I bear a peculiar scar. It has been there since my birth. "Are you quite well, Georgette?"

She quickly moves her hand to her lap like a child caught being naughty. "Oh, yes. I become easily distracted by my thoughts."

"You may speak plainly with me. I have no judgment to cast upon you." I sigh deeply, now plagued by my own thoughts. "Honestly, I envy your position."

"*You* envy *me*?" She laughs. "With all this splendor?" Georgette gestures about the garden. How she must think me a boorish, spoiled woman.

"You have a freedom that is not accessible to me. It is not possible." I shake my head, averting her stare, feeling self-conscious. "You must think me mad. Surrounded by decadence, and yet I complain. I'm a silly woman."

Georgette reaches across the table and lays a hand upon my own. She turns my hand over, revealing fingertips forever blackened by my impossible dreams. "You are no silly woman. We are cursed with artists' hearts in a world built for men. Fear not, ma chère. We will find our way, and it will be the men who fear *us*."

"How does your heart bear it? You create such magnificence, and a man who does not exist receives the accolades and notoriety belonging to you?"

A sly grin crosses her lips. "Ah. So, you have guessed my devious little secret. I knew you were clever." She threads her stained fingers through my own. "Life is a game, Audrey. The men may set the rules, but I was born to break them. What better revenge than success at that which they have fixed in their favor?" She sits back and swirls her wine about her glass. "There are more of us, ma chère." Her demeanor is casual, as though we speak of the weather.

I lean in, eager to learn more of what she speaks, for I cannot help myself. "More of *who*?"

"Women winning the men's game. You, too, can win, Audrey. If only you are bold enough to play." She raises her glass to me, then drinks, never pulling her eyes from my own.

I lie awake long after Georgette has departed, turning our conversation over in my head. She has shattered my understanding of the world—ripped the blindfold from my eyes, and forever changed my vision of the future, my ambition. Do I dare chase the impossible? Do I dare assume a new identity and sell my stories? How will I accomplish such a feat without Charles's knowledge?

His wrath would be unfathomable if he were to find me out. Is it worth the fallout?

It is after midnight when I finally hear my husband's footsteps approach our bedchamber, so I feign being long deep in slumber.

He moves about the room, dressing for bed. I lie quiet and still, praying to any god who may listen that he does not disturb me. The mattress shifts under his weight, and I roll helplessly into his body. He reeks of liquor and something floral that I may presume is courtesy of one of his lovers. I hold my tongue and settle into his warmth, playing the role of the devoted wife to which I am so accustomed.

I am a fraud.

"Audrey." My name passes his lips, deep and husky with drink and smoke, and he slides a hand up my nightdress, skimming my thigh and brushing his fingers between my legs. He has not touched me in an age or uttered my name with such desire in so long I cannot remember. I cannot stop myself, my body reacts of its own volition, and our mouths meet.

I taste her, whoever she is, upon his lips and on his tongue. Charles has done nothing to hide his indiscretion. Her fragrance envelopes me, mingling with the earthiness of tobacco and the sweetness of whiskey. His hubris and audacity set my blood aflame. Yet I play the role. Selfishly and without apology, I seek my pleasure and allow Charles and his traitorous mouth to worship me as I deserve.

With the taste of another woman lingering in my mouth and the feel of a devious man between my legs, I hold his head, fingers laced through his hair as my body writhes and shudders from unyielding waves of pleasure. I force him to remain where he is, locking my legs around his shoulders, my hips undulating with need. As I come undone once more, I reach a state of clarity.

I smile to myself, my decision made: I will be bold.

SCENE FOUR

LONDON

MY PIANOFORTE INSTRUCTOR IS frustrated. I am wholly surprised she has not rapped my knuckles with a paddle for all the mistakes I make. Perhaps I could convince her to deliver a report to Charles that I am hopeless, and this is not time well spent. I bite back a devious grin, and my fingers slip from their position, earning a heavy sigh from Mrs. Danby. "Again, Lady Jameson." Her voice is weary, as though I am a child misbehaving. I give her what I hope is an apologetic look and replay the exercise, careful to repeat my errors at the same places.

At the end of my lesson, I can plainly see that my instructor has acquired a headache. She rubs circles with two fingers at her temples and dramatically moans for effect. Lucy refills her tea, which she downs quickly, eager to depart and move on to a more musically adept student.

I make my apologies to Mrs. Danby with the promise to practice before our next lesson, though I have no intention of touching this blasted instrument unless coaxed to do so by Charles. I breathe a sigh of relief when I hear the front door close. Rising from my seat at the pianoforte, I lift the lid, revealing my new rolls of parchment and the story I began writing this morning after taking care of necessary correspondence and household duties.

I take my place at my desk, wet the nib of my pen with ink, and begin. I feel something unfamiliar spark within myself, and I flush with excitement. My hand moves with fervor across the parchment. The scratching of the nib is a symphony, my words flowing in delicate yet deliberate strokes as my heart's desires take shape.

I jump at a knock on the door and clutch at my chest. "My lady, I didn't mean to startle you. Supper will be served shortly. Your lord husband is expected to join you this evening."

"Thank you, Lucy. I will be along in a moment." I glance about the room and see how the light has shifted. The radiance of the afternoon has dissipated, leaving me in the deep orange glow of the setting sun.

My desk is covered in sheets upon sheets of parchment overflowing with my words. The black stains on my hands are intensified. It is only now that I notice the cramping of my fingers, for I have been writing for hours.

I neatly organize the sheets, carefully rolling and securing them with a bit of twine. Checking to ensure no one is in the hall, I tuck them back into the safety of the piano bench.

I rush to the basin to scrub the evidence from my hands as best I can, but it's no use. Why does it feel as though I have committed a crime? I have done nothing more than commit my thoughts to paper. And yet, my heart thunders against my chest, and I grow short of breath with worry of being discovered. I lean over the basin, knuckles turning white as I grip the table and attempt to regain my composure. "Audrey, you must have courage. Dare to be bold."

As I say my affirmation aloud, I realize a spark of courage does exist in my heart. Perhaps it always did, but I was too blinded by the oppressive forces surrounding me, dictating who I ought to be and how I ought to behave. Those voices are quiet, drowned out by Georgette's forceful command. *You can win, Audrey.*

My fingers relax, and I righten myself. Charles's booming pronouncement that he has arrived home echoes through the foyer. I glance at myself in the mirror and tuck stray bits of hair back into place. There is a fire in my eyes that did not exist before today. With my head held high, I float downstairs to dinner with a new lightness in my heart.

Charles announces at dinner that he will depart in the morning. A duke has requested his presence to discuss business affairs. He will join him at his estate for the week. "Robert is packing my belongings as we speak." He neatly cuts a portion of beef and brings it to his mouth— his mouth that I cannot help but stare at, wondering who it will please in the week to come. I am not so naïve as to believe he will be faithful after our tryst last evening.

I sip my wine and smile wistfully across the table as a good little wife should. "Can you not shorten your excursion? A week is so very long, my dear Charles."

He sighs, heavy with annoyance. "Audrey, darling, I cannot expect you to understand the criticality of my presence at his estate. He requires my full attention to settle his affairs. Besides, you have much with which you can busy yourself. I will ask Mrs. Danby to visit an extra day while I am gone. Perhaps a visit with your mother and father is in order."

My grip on my knife tightens as he talks down to me, as though I am a simpleton who cannot appreciate how the dealings of men work. I force a pout. "I know. You have been so dedicated to your work, it's just that I miss you so."

His expression softens, and he dabs the corners of his mouth with his napkin and places it on the table next to his platter. "Once I return, I promise, I will make time for you. I will speak with Robert and have him make arrangements for a short holiday at my father's country estate. We have not visited in an age."

I dip my head in thanks. "That sounds wonderful."

Charles's usual critical stare is rearranged into an expression I do not recognize and cannot discern. "And, perhaps, it is time for you to produce an heir."

An *heir*?

I nearly topple from my chair. I knew this conversation would eventually need to be had, but a small part of me hoped Charles would not wish for a child for some time to come. Or perhaps he would simply decide he did not want children. He certainly does not have the disposition or patience for a child.

What a foolish thought.

I am a terrible woman for not wishing to give my husband children, but the thought of bearing as many children as it will take to give him a male heir, if not multiple sons, feels crushing. It feels like a death sentence, further cementing me into this life that I resent and abhor.

With a different man in other circumstances, a family would be lovely. In a life where I have a doting husband who cherishes me, who would be a loving father.

That man is not Charles.

The grin on my face feels foreign as I feign excitement. "Oh, Charles," is all I manage to say.

He rises from the table. "I must retire to my study. There is much to prepare before I depart."

I nod once more. He rounds the table and places a quick kiss upon my cheek before quitting the room.

Finally, left to myself, I slump in my chair and down my wine. I take note of more soulless paintings hung about the room. Perhaps another visit to Georgette is in order.

SCENE FIVE

LONDON

GEORGETTE IS IN THE back of the gallery, preparing two paintings for delivery to my home. As we settle the payment, an idea occurs to me. "Georgette, my husband's work has taken him away for the week. I'd love to invite you to stay as my guest for a few days."

"As your guest?"

"Yes. You wished to paint in my gardens. This is the perfect opportunity."

Her face lights up at the mention of painting, and I know she wishes to accept my invitation. "Are you sure, ma chère?"

"Do not give it another thought. My days grow lonely, and I can only feign interest in the pianoforte for so many hours." I roll my eyes, and Georgette giggles and gives a little snort.

"You cannot possibly be as terrible as you have stated."

I place a hand on her shoulder and lean in earnestly. "My dear, you have not yet heard me play. I assure you, your ears will beg of me to stop."

My new friend snorts another laugh. We speak for a few minutes more to finalize our plans for the week. Brimming with excited energy, I walk through town toward my home, passing by women who whisper behind their hands about me. They no doubt spread rumors of my husband's rakish behavior, but I cannot be bothered to care today. Let them talk.

The curious scar upon my breast tugs with fevered intensity the further from the gallery I move. It is not unpleasant. It feels as though it is guiding me.

When I arrive home, I send Robert to bring Georgette and her belongings while Lucy prepares a guest suite for her stay. Two hours later, Georgette and I are enjoying tea and cakes in the drawing room, and my newly acquired paintings are in the process of being displayed in the dining room.

The weather turns, and a storm blows in, disrupting our plans to take our supper on the terrace. Instead, I have Lucy serve us in the drawing room. We finish an entire bottle of wine, and I ask one of the maids to bring us a second, not caring to conduct myself with a modicum of decorum. Sitting by the fire in our stocking feet, I feel more content than I can ever recall since before Charles and I wed.

I long for the life I led before promenades through the park with Charles during our courtship. Balls and tea with other ladies in the neighborhood are a bore. Sprawled on the floor with Georgette, impaired by drink and laughing at tales from her travels, I feel whole. The ache of loneliness is replaced with something new: sisterhood.

It must be a trick of the light or perhaps my inebriation, but a soft halo of white light surrounds us.

Georgette refills our glasses and gestures hers toward the pianoforte. Her cheeks are rosy, and she hiccups a little. "Audrey, you *must* play for me."

I am sitting against the divan, legs stretched out before me, dress bunched up around my middle in the most unbecoming manner. Crumbs from our tea cakes litter the floor around me, and I can feel them down my dress. Thunder softly rumbles in the distance, and the pitter-patter of rain drums against the windows. "You cannot be serious. I am dreadful *without* drink. I am not certain I could manage to read the music right now."

Georgette pulls herself to her feet and begins her search through my sheet music for a song. She finds one she deems acceptable and sits at the bench, patting the seat beside her. "Come now, Audrey. Be a good host and play a song for me."

Groaning with feigned exasperation, I make my way to her, a little unsteady on my feet and feeling flush from the wine. Georgette wears a gleeful expression as I place my fingers upon the keys. It takes me but a few notes before I make an error. I wish my inebriation were the cause of my persistent errors, but I know better. I haven't the heart, nor the coordination, for this.

After a few minutes, a soft hand grasps one of my own. Georgette's shoulders shake with uncontrollable laughter. "Audrey. Ma chère." She gives me a pitying look, but her sapphire eyes sparkle with mirth. "You truly are dreadful. You must swear *never* to touch this instrument again. It is not for you, darling." She pats my hand affectionately, and I can no longer contain my own giggles. I lean into Georgette, our heads bent together with tears streaming down our faces. My cheeks ache from smiling.

It is a foreign feeling to be filled with such elation.

Yet, it feels right.

That strange tug in my chest returns, followed by a sense of déjà vu. This all seems so familiar, and I cannot place my finger on why. I have no sisters, and friends have not come so easily. This experience with Georgette is wholly new and exciting.

I realize for the first time in my life that I may finally have a friend, a confidant.

I nudge Georgette to stand. "I want to share something I have been working on with you. But you must promise to speak of it to no one."

Her eyebrows arch with curiosity. "I am intrigued." She moves from the bench so I may lift the lid, exposing neatly tied parchment rolls containing my stories. I select one and hold it protectively to my chest.

"Now, you must promise not to cast judgment upon me. Your words the other night… they woke something within me. I do not wish to be this pitiful creature who nods and behaves as her husband and society expect. I want to be courageous, like you. I want to take chances." My heart races within my chest, and I cannot contain my excitement nor my nervousness as I hand the bundle of parchment to my friend. She takes it carefully and sits on the divan, legs tucked under her.

I monitor her expression. It shifts from concentration, brows furrowed, to eyebrows raised and biting her lip. She steals a glance at me and returns to her reading. The wait for her reaction is agonizing. My confidence falters as the minutes that feel like an eternity silently pass us by.

I anxiously pace about the room, biting at my thumbnail. Finally, the fluttering of pages breaks the silence. "Audrey, ma chère."

"Is it awful?" I wince, eager to hear her criticism so that I may move on.

"It is… what is the English word… *salacious*."

I bury my head in my hands, filled with shame. "It was ridiculous of me to write such filth. I have forgotten myself. Where is my head, Georgette?" Panic seizes me, and my hands fly to my mouth. "What if Charles finds me out?"

"Audrey, please cease your pacing. It's doing my head in." She closes her eyes and sighs. "Come, sit by me." I smooth my dress and sink into the divan. Sitting up straight, Georgette lightly pats my knee, drawing my attention. "What you have created is magnificent. This," she shakes the pages at me, "is bold. It is brazen. It is what women thirst for but may not speak aloud. It is what we long for and yet all we are granted is a man who uses us for his own pleasure before turning away and leaving us wanting."

Her words penetrate my mind and my soul. The glow about us returns, but this time, she seems to take note of it as well, placing a hand to her chest. "I believe it may be time to retire for the evening."

Disappointed by the end of our evening, I sigh. "Yes, I suppose you are right. I'll send Lucy along to stoke the fire in your room."

She rolls the parchment and places it back in the bench with the rest of my secrets. When she reaches the threshold, she hesitates and turns to me. "You are remarkable, Audrey. Do not snuff out this flame. It suits you." She smiles warmly and leaves me for the night.

SCENE SIX

LONDON

THE NEXT MORNING, THE skies are clear of the previous evening's storms, replaced by the sun's resplendent cheer. Lucy lays several blankets on the lawn and leaves Georgette and me with a basket of pastries, fruit, and cheeses to graze on throughout the morning.

Georgette is seated on a stool at her easel and canvas, deep in concentration. I marvel at her. She is consumed with her work, barely glancing up from her canvas except to briefly observe some spot unknown to me in the garden before disappearing back into her own world.

I leave her be, curling up on my blanket with a book in hand. I have read this tale before, of the knight and peasant girl, but it brings me comfort, so I read it again, losing myself in the story.

Imagining, once more, that I am the peasant girl, consumed by the love of a man who cares nothing for dowries and balls and titles.

When I finish my book, I lean back against my favorite tree and close my eyes, allowing another dream to take hold: one where I do not covet the love nor the approval of a man. I dream of a life where my fate is my own and my days are filled with conversations with other women who answer to no man. In this life, I wear the stains upon my hands with honor.

In the comfort of Georgette's company, I allow the midday heat to lull me to sleep in the sanctuary of my tree.

SCENE SEVEN

LONDON

"GEORGETTE," I GASP. "THIS is stunning!"

I study the painting she spent the day creating while I read and wasted away. She perfectly captured the pond. I can almost see the branches of the weeping willows gently blowing in the breeze, with light filtering through their branches and reflecting off of the pond's rippling surface.

"Merci, ma chère. Your garden is truly inspiring in its tranquility."

I nudge her playfully. "If I did not know better, Georgette, I would think you are more enamored with my garden than our friendship."

She nudges me back. "Oh, Audrey. I came for the garden, but I stayed for the scandalous reading material." Georgette's nose wrinkles as she sharply exhales through it, unable to keep a straight face.

"You are wicked!" I playfully flick her nose.

She waves her hand dismissively. "Oh, I know. I cannot help it, nor will I apologize for it. I am a woman who knows what she wants."

I link my arm through hers and nudge her to walk back toward the house for us to clean up for dinner. "I would not have you any other way."

That evening, we retire again to the drawing room, this time with tea and cakes rather than wine. Georgette is flung across the divan, reading more of my stories while I sit at my desk, writing a new piece.

But this one is different from the love stories Georgette is greedily consuming.

In this story, two women embark on an adventure, free of the constraints of society's patriarchal binds. They spend their days exploring new towns and their nights creating works of art, singing in taverns, and taking lovers without guilt or shame.

They live a life untethered to the expectations of men who do not care for them.

They live the life I desire with every beat of my heart.

I stay up long after Georgette has retired for the evening, filling pages with the story of us: the story of what could be.

My scar thrums happily, contented by the grand dreams I weave. I write until my inkwell runs dry.

And so, the story of Marcella and Chiara blooms to life.

SCENE EIGHT

LONDON

"AUDREY?"

I startle awake, squinting against the harsh morning light, disoriented by my surroundings. Parchment sticks to my sweat-slicked face, which Georgette delicately peels away. I glance around, a bit dazed. "Good gracious! Did I sleep in the drawing room?" I wipe at the crusted moisture at the corners of my mouth, embarrassed to be found in such a state.

Georgette chuckles gently. "It would appear you were… what is the phrase? Burning the midnight oil?"

I fuss with my hair, which has fallen out of its pins, combing out the tangles with my fingers. "I must look a fright."

The door creaks, and Georgette and I turn to see Lucy standing in the doorway, looking sheepish. "My lady? Are you well? Should I send for the doctor?"

"No, Lucy, that will not be necessary. Can you please fetch breakfast? I'll attend to dressing myself this morning."

"Yes, my lady." She curtsies and hurries to the kitchens.

When she is out of range of hearing, I jump up from my seat. "Goodness, what a disaster. What if she tells Charles?" I struggle, trying to reach the laces behind my back, suddenly feeling suffocated by the corset. "Blast it! Georgette, can you please help me get out of this ridiculous dress?"

"Audrey, you must calm down. Let's go to your room, and we will set you right."

While I clean myself at the wash-basin, Georgette explores my wardrobe, trying on hats and inspecting my dresses. "Audrey, darling. Do you have any dresses that are less… confining?"

Patting my face dry, I glance at my friend, who is donning a ridiculous, large-brimmed hat that my mother gifted me. She wears it tilted at an angle so that it hides half of her face. "No. Why?"

"It seems impractical to dress in this way every day. It's a small wonder you can breathe at all." She holds up a gown with a particularly stiff bodice. "Shall I bind you, ma chère?" She raises her eyebrows at me with a devilish grin.

I study Georgette's own dress. Her cerulean skirt is light and moves freely, and is paired with a cream chemise and floral stays. It looks much more comfortable than the layers of fabric that Lucy laces me into daily. I bite my lip in thought. What if I were to dress as Georgette? I quickly dismiss the thought, knowing Charles would be appalled to see me dressed in what he would consider peasants' clothes. As if I do not already elicit enough gossip among the other noble wives, this would certainly bring much dishonor to Charles and his precious reputation.

Everything I am is as directed by the will of others: Charles, my mother, and my father. The girl who climbed trees, who ran wild and free, has been locked away in the recesses of my mind and my heart, and all she wants is to escape. She just wants to be loved as she is— not told that she is wrong for merely existing.

I am so consumed by indignation, the world around me fades, replaced by a roaring in my ears. A rage that has been slowly percolating beneath the surface of my consciousness builds to a crescendo, threatening to destroy me.

My clothes suddenly feel like restraints, meant to subdue me. They are a sign of the power men hold over me, dictating what defines me as a woman.

My breath comes quick and ragged in my fury. Standing here in nothing more than a chemise and dressing gown, I am suddenly too hot from this fire raging within me. I tear off the dressing gown and cast it to the floor. A raw sob of frustration threatens to choke me.

"Audrey? Audrey!" Georgette's hands grasp my shoulders and shake me. Her crystal eyes are clouded with worry.

"I can't... breathe." Grasping at my heaving chest, the sob finally breaks free. I fall into Georgette's arms, and for possibly the first time in my life, I feel safe. She carefully guides me down to the floor, pulling me into a fierce embrace. She doesn't say a word beyond calming shushing sounds as she gently rocks me in her arms as though I am a child.

We stay there until the well of my despair has run dry, and I have no more tears left to cry. At some point, she had sent Lucy away, asking her to leave the tray of food in the hall.

I am lying with my head in Georgette's lap while she runs her fingers through my hair, when I finally gain the courage to speak. "I am a prisoner in my own home, Georgette. In my own life. I do not know how I can continue to bear it." My voice is a raspy whisper, my throat dry and raw from crying.

I feel her shift beneath my head. "Up. Sit up." I do as she bids, and her hands grip the sides of my face. "*You* are powerful. You will bear it by *winning* this game. Write your stories. Print your stories and sell them by whatever means you can. Your words will be your salvation and your freedom."

Her words reignite the flame within my heart.

Bold, Audrey. Be bold.

SCENE NINE

LONDON

THE HOUSE FEELS EMPTY without Georgette. After my breakdown, we spent an additional day lazing about the gardens, reading, writing, and painting. I wish our time together did not have to come to an end, but Georgette's gallery needed her attention. I had sent word to Mrs. Danby that I was unwell, canceling my lessons for the week and allowing me to spend all of my time with my friend. I am certain Mrs. Danby was all too pleased to be relieved of my appalling piano playing.

Georgette must have painted five or six landscapes of the property, gifting me one. It's breathtaking. I am seated under a weeping willow on a blanket with a book in hand. Sunbeams filter through the branches, highlighting my face.

I had planned to gift it to Charles for his study, but instead decided to keep the painting for myself and hang it in the drawing room. It represents a piece of me that Charles does not care to understand: the piece of me that has agency over her dreams, even if she cannot claim them as her own.

If Georgette can be content selling her art under the name of a man, I can do the same.

And I will.

Charles is expected tomorrow, and I am conflicted on his return. His talk of beginning a family weighs heavily on my mind. It feels like one more burden to carry upon my shoulders, one more obligation that threatens to destroy me.

Or, could this possibly be a turning point for Charles and me? Could a child soften his rough edges? Could a child open his heart?

A voice echoes in my head, warning me to guard my heart. Has Charles not already shown me that he does not truly care for me after all these years? Am I still nothing more than a business deal with my father?

I cannot bear to sit here thinking these thoughts. It will drive me mad. And so, I decide to take a turn about town. There is a warm breeze, and the sun shines brilliantly. I tilt my hat to avoid the glare as I complete my errands, stopping by the bookshop and the patisserie. I take the long way home, stopping by Georgette's gallery with a gift of raspberry tarts.

When I enter, I am stunned to find the walls bare. "Georgette?" I call out, my voice echoing about the space. She appears from the back room, beads of sweat gleaming across her forehead. Her twisted hair is rumpled and coming undone. "Oh, Audrey. I am so pleased you stopped by. I have not had a moment to reach out."

"What is happening?"

Her face falls, and for the first time since she came into my life, she looks abashed. "Oh, *ma chère*, I must return to Le Mans. I leave in just a few days." Her voice is quiet, lacking her usual bravado. Her hand rubs at her chest, as I have so often seen her do these past few weeks when she seems distressed.

My stomach plummets. No. This cannot be. "Must you? So soon?"

"I am afraid so. I do not stay in one place for very long. I will spend the remainder of the season in Le Mans before moving to Paris. The demand for an original Bonnet in Paris has captured my attention. My gallery will open before the holidays.

I swipe at my eyes, willing myself not to fall apart when wondrous things are happening for my friend. I pull Georgette into an embrace. "Oh, Georgette, that is wonderful! And so well deserved."

"This has been my dream for so long. I can hardly believe it is happening!" Her hands cover her cheeks in shock. Her expression then turns solemn. "But, Audrey, I will miss you so. You have been a true and dear friend to me for the short time our lives have crossed paths."

At that, my heart begins to fissure and break into pieces. My only friend is leaving, and I will return to my solitude. Georgette takes my face in her hands and wipes the moisture from my cheeks. "Darling, do not cry, for you will make me cry as well."

"I apologize. I am so very happy for you. It is just so odd. I feel as though I have always known you, and now, you must leave. It seems unfair."

"Come with me." The invitation spills from her lips quickly.

I blanche at Georgette. I cannot have heard her correctly. "Come with you?"

She bites her bottom lip and nods furiously. "Oui! Why not? You are miserable in this life. You are miserable in this marriage that oppresses you and holds you back from how brilliant you are. Come with me. We will have adventures and find romance with handsome Parisian men. We will be successful, selling our art and our stories. We'll want for nothing! Be *bold*, Audrey. Be audacious!"

I walk about the empty gallery, fisting my hands through my hair and pulling it free from its pins. "Georgette, what you speak of is madness! I am *married*. Charles returns home tomorrow. I cannot leave. I have no means beyond Charles to pay my way. And what of my parents? The scandal is too great."

Georgette captures my hand and spins me toward her. "Audrey, look at me. *You* can do this. My carriage departs for the coast first thing Sunday. Pack whatever you can and bring it to me this afternoon. You shine too brightly for a life in the dark." Her eager eyes implore me to give in. But how can I? How can I even remove my belongings from my home without notice? How can I leave the only life I know?

I swallow the aching lump gathered in my throat. My eyes burn with the salt of my sorrow that I shall never see Georgette again after this day. I envelope her in my arms and kiss each of her cheeks before tearing myself from her. "I am sorry, Georgette. It's impossible. I wish you all the happiness in the world, my dear friend."

Before she can protest, I rush from the gallery, my heart heavy with inconceivable loss.

SCENE TEN

LONDON

CHARLES RETURNED THIS MORNING, but quickly departed for his office. He must have traveled straight through the night. He stayed long enough to bathe and change from his travel clothes. He barely took note of me, solidifying every poor thought I had about his return.

I have spent the day in our suite, making my excuses to Lucy that I am with headache. She brought me tea and a platter of bread and cheese for lunch. Otherwise, I have been left to myself, lying in bed with a book.

It is late afternoon when I finally force myself from my melancholy and dress for dinner. Lucy laces me into a beautiful dress, green as a pine forest. I decide to wear jewels to dinner. Emeralds that belonged to my grandmother dangle from my ears.

To my surprise, Charles is already seated when I make my way to the dining room. He is reading the Oxford Gazette and drinking brandy. He looks up from his reading just long enough to take note of my presence. "Audrey, you look lovely this evening." I pause by his chair long enough to kiss his cheek before claiming my seat across the table.

"How was your trip? Everything went well?"

His face remains buried behind his paper. My nails bite into my palm. My husband has been gone for a week and cannot grant me a moment of his attention. He acts as though his time is the most precious in the world, and I am to sit here and wait patiently for him to dish out his affections.

"Yes, yes. I am told you canceled your lessons with Mrs. Danby this week." He peers over the top of his paper at me, eyes creased with suspicion.

I wave a hand, as though it is of no consequence. "I was not feeling up to it."

At this, he lowers his paper, glowering at me. "I have paid Mrs. Danby a most generous sum. The least you can do is keep your appointments. You were not feeling well enough to complete your lessons, yet I am told you were well enough to host a guest in my absence?"

I sip my wine, trying to remain calm. "It is my home, too, Charles. Am I to spend all of my time in solitude, waiting for you to decide I am worthy of your time?" The words fall from my mouth before I can stop them.

Red creeps up Charles's face, and his nostrils flare in challenge. "You forget your place, *wife*." He spits the word 'wife' like poison. "*I* am *Lord* of this household. It is good enough for you to spend my hard-earned coin on this ridiculous art and stuffing yourself like a pig with pastries. You will speak to me with reverence and respect."

My breath is caught in my throat. I am afraid to move, to speak another word. His cruelty cuts through me like a knife. "I apologize, *my lord*. It is only that I miss you when you are away." I loathe the tears prickling my eyes, but not as much as I loathe myself for groveling for his forgiveness for speaking the truth of my heart. I loathe the lie that drips from my lips like a balm to soothe his ego.

We eat the rest of our meal in silence, and I retire to the drawing room and he to his study, as we are accustomed. I am seated on the divan, halfheartedly working on a needlepoint of lilacs when Charles enters. I smell the tobacco and brandy before I see him standing before me. I look up from my work and say nothing, waiting for him to explain his presence.

He gestures to the empty spot next to me, and I shift slightly closer to the edge of the divan, making room for him. He sits and sighs. "Audrey, my darling. I must apologize for my behavior. I was weary from travel, and your disrespect cut through me. Please do better in the future to mind your manners, and we can put this messy business behind us."

I do not want his apology, if you could call his words an apology; I only want him to leave me in peace. Playing into this charade is the only way out. "Thank you, Charles." He pats my knee but does not remove his hand. I want to recoil from his touch, but instead, I place my own hand atop his.

He squeezes my knee, but his grip does not feel loving: it is a warning for me to fall in line. "Would you play something for me?"

I set my needlework aside. "Of course, my lord."

Satisfied with my deference, he gives me a cutting grin and follows me to the pianoforte, leaning against it as I situate myself and select a song to play. I have barely started to play when something catches my eye. A mouse runs toward me, and I leap from my seat, knocking over the bench. I cry out, trying to explain my actions to Charles, but his attention is elsewhere.

Rolls of parchment are strewn about the floor. An inkwell lies shattered, a black puddle pooling on the rug. "Oh! I'll call Lucy to help clean this straight away." I try to leave, but his hand catches my wrist and yanks me back.

"What is all of this, Audrey?"

I laugh nervously. "It's nothing, Charles. Just some silly stories and poems."

His steely gaze is cold, and the muscle in his jaw ticks. I feel weak, and my stomach turns on itself. "Have a seat, *wife*." His words are hard, unfeeling. Helpless to stop what is about to happen, I take my seat in the nearest chair and fold my hands in my lap, trying desperately to stop their shaking.

The crinkle of parchment is deafening against the eerie quiet in the room as his eyes dart back and forth across the page, his expression unreadable. But his hands clench the pages, knuckles white from his grip. "Charles," I whisper. "If you'll allow me to explain."

Charles closes his eyes and inhales deeply. When his eyes reopen, they are pure fury. "Have you completely lost your senses, Audrey?" He shakes the pages at me. "You *dare* bring this scandal upon my household?

If it weren't for me, you would be *nothing*. You had no prospects, but your father *assured* me you would be a good and compliant wife. You have been nothing but trouble from the start. I am a generous man. I permit you to spend my money however you please, spend your days wasting away in the most undignified and unbecoming manner of a lady of the estate, and *this* is how you repay me?" His voice booms like thunder. Spittle flies from his mouth, his eyes bulging in a fit of rage.

He wrenches me from my seat and brings our faces together. His hot breath reeks from his pipe and drink. He still holds my story in his other hand, and I cannot tear my eyes from it. He shakes me, and I meet his eyes. "I am a man of honor, Audrey. This is a scandal we would *never* recover from. You are an ungrateful, deceitful woman, and I will not have this in my household."

At this, I break. "*Honor?*" I choke out the word, practically laughing. "You sleep with your mistresses and then dare come home to *our* bed and put your mouth on me with the taste of them still on your disgusting tongue, and you *dare* speak to me of honor?"

Before I know what is happening, my face explodes with pain. Stars dance in my vision, and the floor rushes up to meet me. Moaning, I watch as Charles flings my stories into the fireplace. "No!" I crawl to the fireplace and watch the parchment curl and burn to ash in the flames. Bent over myself, I sob at my loss as he tosses each parchment roll into the merrily crackling hearth. My head throbs, and the metallic tang of my blood fills my mouth.

Charles looms over me, wiping my blood from his fingers with a handkerchief which he then casts into the flames to burn among my hopes and my dreams. "You will not engage in this activity again. If I find a single sheet of parchment bearing these sinful thoughts, you will be on the next carriage to the sanitarium. Do I make myself clear, *wife*?"

I can only nod my head. His footsteps grow distant, and I collapse on the floor.

SCENE ELEVEN

LONDON

CHARLES LEFT LAST NIGHT. I suspect he went to one of his mistresses. The side of my face is swollen and purple with bruises, the corner of my lip split open. I gingerly cleanse my face, the sting and pain so great it takes all of my effort not to empty my stomach of its meager contents from the nausea.

Lucy tiptoes around me, going about her duties, but saying nothing. I do not even have it in my heart to feel betrayed by Lucy and Robert, as their salaries come from Charles. They are not beholden to me. They owe me no loyalty.

I am officially on my own.

And I know what I must do.

I pull one of my travel bags from my wardrobe and fill it with just the essentials. Two of my least restrictive dresses, a coat, undergarments, and a few family heirlooms. In my second bag, I store my jewels and my precious few books. I creep out into the hall and listen for any movement about the house. Lucy is at the market, and Robert is on an errand for Charles. I do not have much time.

I steal away into Charles's office and move aside a grim painting of Charles's father on the wall behind his desk, revealing his safe. Tugging on the handle, I breathe a sigh of relief that it is unlocked. I open it to find stacks of notes and coins. I help myself to what I consider adequate penance for laying his hands on me and burning my stories: I take it all.

Hastily, I finish packing my things and leave the house. With a hat pulled low over the injured side of my face, I walk as quickly as I can to the gallery. The building is empty, and the door is locked. "No. No! She isn't to leave until tomorrow!" I step back from the building and set my bags down. The tugging at my chest begins then. The pull is sharp, urgent. I grasp at my chest, and my heart pounds with the fury of a horse galloping at full speed.

I feel faint and quickly step back toward the building, bracing myself against the cool glass of the front window. Last evening replays over and over in my head.

I had lain by the fire for hours, long after my manuscripts had shriveled and disintegrated to ash. Charles laying his hands upon me is but a trifle of my concern. He has done so before when I displeased him with my odd ways. The hollowness of my heart pulses with need, a tugging sensation that persists as though a rope is looped around my heart, urging me to keep moving forward. I have nothing left to lose, so I pick up my bags and walk.

As I move down the road, the sensation quickens, and I know deep in my gut that I am moving toward something important. Suddenly, my vision is obscured by a burst of brilliant light. Flashes of two young women cross my mind. It is as though I am watching the story of their lives before my very eyes. Dancing in a village square. Draped in black with tears staining their cheeks. Laughing with empty goblets nearby. Bent over a table in concentration. Tied to posts. Flames.

I stumble as I practically feel the flames licking at my face, my breath caught in my throat. A gentleman stops and places a hand on my back. "My lady, are you well?"

I do not know how to answer him. Tears flow down my cheeks, and I am overwhelmed by a barrage of emotion and memories weaving their way through my body.

I quickly brush him away, the urgent need to find my sister taking hold. "Yes, yes." I rush. "Thank you, kindly. I apologize, I must go."

My feet carry me faster than I have run since I was a child toward the hotel two blocks away. I know it is where I must go, without a shadow of doubt. I must make it to the hotel.

I am a block away when a laugh bursts from within. Elation as I have never known in all my life thrums through my body. When I arrive, I walk right past the front desk and up the stairs in search of the missing piece of my heart. I knock on the door at the end of the hall in a quick tempo, unable to contain myself until finally she answers.

She opens the door and immediately takes notice of the state of my face and gasps, ushering me into her room. She closes the door behind her, and I throw myself into her arms. "Chiara." I breathe her name. Her true name. The name I knew so very long ago.

My sister's body stiffens in my arms. Slowly, she unwinds herself from my embrace and steps back, studying me like a puzzle she is struggling to solve. Her brows are knit together, and she chews on her bottom lip.

I am quiet, allowing her time to piece together the truth of our relationship. The muscles in her face relax, and her hands cover her mouth, a sob catching before she envelops me once more. "Marcella. Oh, Marcella. My sister." Her body trembles with her weeping. Her fingers dig into my back as we cling to one another.

After another moment, I pull from her hold and cup her face in my hands. She bends her head to rest her forehead upon my own. "I promised I would find you," I whisper. "I promised."

"My heart, Marcella. My heart beats once more for us both." She pushes down the top of her dress, exposing the starburst scar that mirrors my own. "I finally feel as though I can truly breathe. Your soul has returned to me."

The familiar thump of Chiara's heart beats in time with my own, and I am whole for the first time in this life.

She brushes a hand over my bruised face. "Charles? He did this to you?"

I nod. "Chiara, I wish to be bold. I wish to be brave."

A mischievous grin spreads across her face. "Then our adventure begins in Paris."

SCENE TWELVE

ENGLISH CHANNEL

THE CARRIAGE RIDE TO Dover was perilous. It took just over a day, with a stop at an inn to rest and water the horses. Charles's money could have paid for us to stay in our own rooms, but we chose to share, not wanting to be apart for even a moment now that we are finally together again.

Now that we are finally whole.

It is just as we were in my bed in my family cottage in Montefioralle. We talked all night about our plans for our life together in Paris. We will stay in Le Mans at her family's home for a month or so before we depart for the city.

It is too painful to speak of the horrors that ended our lives in our village in Italy. We instead focus on the future. We have been blessed by the All Mother to find one another in our rebirth, just as the spell intended.

I stand by the bow of the ship that sails for France, writing in a journal I purchased the day before in the small town where we had rested. I feel the moment Chiara joins me, and my heart leaps with joy at her presence. She rests her forearms on the side of the small ship we chartered and sighs dreamily as the coast comes into view. The sky is streaked with hues of orange and pink, and I know she longs to capture the view in a painting. And she will.

I close my journal and stow it in my skirts. "What are you thinking, cara mia?"

She sighs again. "I am thinking that it will be good to not share a bed with you again tonight. You still snore something fierce."

"And you still snort when you laugh like a little piglet happy he has found a truffle."

Chiara's sharp elbow digs into my side, and I cry out, then elbow her back. "Well, we are off to a fantastic start to our new life, ma sorella. Your ability to pick at my nerves has not faded with time."

I lean over and kiss her temple, smiling into her tangle of curls. "It has not."

She leans her head on my shoulder, and we stare at our future home looming on the horizon.

ACT THREE

PARIS, FRANCE

APRIL 1796

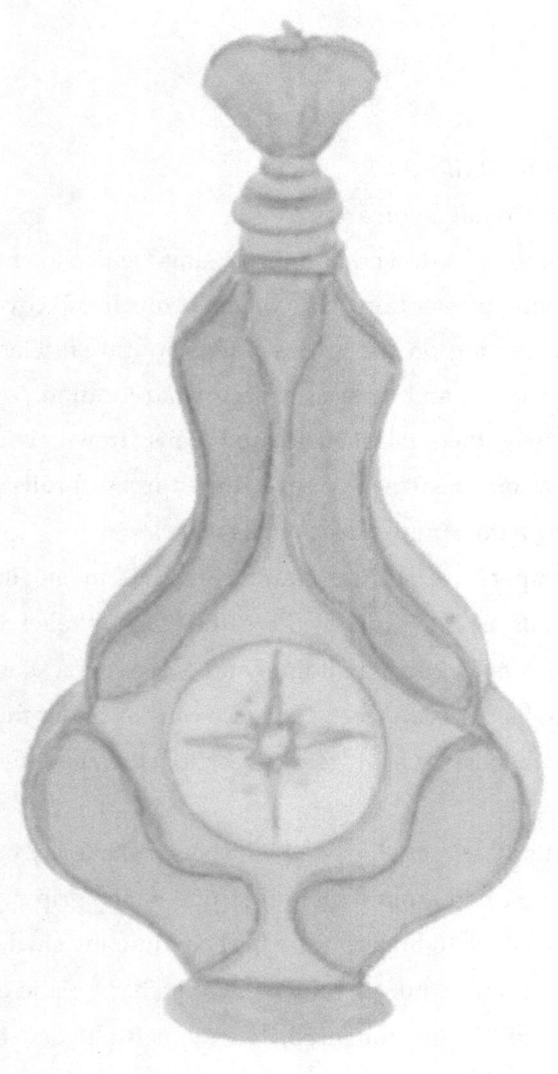

SCENE ONE

PARIS

BOOM! BOOM! BOOM!

"Get down!" Tomas commands.

The walls of the run-down inn on Rue Saint-Denis violently shake—dust and crumbling plaster rain down on us. I crouch and cover my head with my arms, choking on the grit invading my throat. Gerard rushes about, snuffing candles and lanterns to secure our location. My husband, Laurence, quickly gathers the sketches and plans strewn about the table and shoves them into a satchel. An overturned inkwell rolls past me on the floor, leaving a thick trail of black in its wake.

Once the papers are secure, Laurence comes to me in the pitch darkness and pulls me into his body. I breathe a sigh of relief at his touch. Another mortar hits a nearby building, and a beam cracks and loosens from the ceiling. Before I can react, Laurence rolls us under the table, and the beam narrowly misses us. My teeth gnash together, and my elbow hits the floor hard.

"Are you hurt, Cat?" my husband whispers. I shake my head against him. His body is curled around me; his strong hands grip my back and head, holding me flush to him, turning his body into my shield.

I return his embrace, burying my face in the hard plane of his chest. "Non, mon amour." I am uninjured, but more frightened than I dare admit. We are all afraid, silently praying to whoever will listen to live through this ceaseless bombardment by the French Royal Army.

Our friends in the resistance surround us, scattered to the corners of the room, taking cover wherever they can. We believed this district of Paris to be secure for our meeting, but we were wrong. Someone in the neighborhood must have let word slip of our meetings.

Time comes to a halt in the silence that follows the barrage of mortars and gunfire, but I hear their unsteady breaths as we anticipate the next strike. Our collective tension is suffocating.

Even in the dark, I can faintly make out the auras of our companions, but there is only one I search for as I peek to the side: Odette. My best friend's familiar leaf green cloud floats like an apparition a few feet away, alongside her husband, Olivier, and our friend, Jacquette.

Laurence's hold on me tightens, and I realize I am trembling. His lips press against the top of my head, and he gently strokes my tangled hair. "I have you, mon étoile. I have you." The deep timber of my husband's voice is soft as he reassures me of his protection.

Long minutes that feel like hours pass by. The silence is unsettling, as if all life has been erased from the world. All we can do is wait with bated breath and hope that if another strike comes, it is not our end.

I silently pray to the All Mother for her strength and protection against the Royal Army's assault.

Laurence's heart pounds fiercely

Floorboards creak under the weight of someone inching toward the window. Gerard, our leader, dares to peer out, keeping to the shadows. I wait with bated breath. "It is done." Gerard's resonant voice does not carry confidence as he whispers his decree.

Laurence's touch recedes, and he helps me climb from under the table. I pull tiny chunks of debris from my hair, shaking out untamed tresses, and hastily brush the dust from my skirt. One of the men lights a lantern, and we gather our belongings.

"Cat!" Odette rushes to me. Her russet eyes are wild with emotion.

I open my arms, and am instantly consumed by her warmth.

"Are you unharmed?" she asks as she pushes my curls from my face, studying me for injury, always the caretaker as our nurse.

"Oui. They've never come that close before. We are lucky."

Her husband, Olivier, comes to us and takes her hand. He offers me a kind smile, his eyes crinkling at the corners. "Ladies, we must leave. Do you have your effects?" Odette is clutching her bag of medical supplies, and I look about the room for Laurence. He has both of our bags.

"Oui. Where shall we go? Are we sure the streets are safe for travel?" I inquire.

My husband and Tomas, one of our scouts, join us. I take my travel bag and heft it onto my shoulder. It clinks from tiny glass bottles jostling around. Laurence and I own a parfumerie in the heart of Paris, but many of the plants I use to create our fragrances have medicinal properties. I keep Odette stocked with remedies and salves for treating injuries and illnesses.

My remedies are special, though, unlike what one would purchase from any apothecary in town.

Tomas responds in a hushed tone, "Get to the cathedral down the block. There is an exit beneath the sanctuary that leads through the sewers. I know the way to my home from there. My house is small, but we should be safe there." We all nod our agreement and file out of the crumbling room.

The stairs are precarious— they are littered with debris, and one of the steps is smashed through. The creaking under our weight fills me with anxiety. Laurence traverses the gap in the stairs, then takes my hands to keep me steady as I carefully hop down to meet him.

At last, we make it to the lobby. Thankfully, it is empty. Other guests have either fled or are still hunkered in their rooms. Gerard glances outside, then motions for us to gather near the stairs, where we are out of sight from the window.

"A few soldiers are outside surveying the area," he informs us. "It will look suspicious if we all leave at once through the front. Laurence and Marie Catherine, you will leave first. Tomas, Claude, and Jacquette exit through the back into the alley. Olivier, wait here with Odette. I will leave with you in thirty minutes."

Gerard checks his pocket watch. "We meet inside the cathedral. We will leave in an hour for Tomas's home. If you do not make it..." His words trail off as he swallows. "We must leave you behind, mes amis."

We do not protest. We understand that which is unspoken: if we are captured, if we are arrested, we are on our own. It must be this way.

Laurence takes my hand, and I welcome the strength I draw from him. I glance over my shoulder at Odette. She catches my eye and gives me an encouraging smile.

We will reunite soon, her eyes promise. I know it as surely as I know my own heartbeat.

I cannot explain our connection. Something inside me is drawn to her, and I feel more whole in her presence. It is different from the love I feel for my husband or my family, and it is difficult to put into words. I am uncertain if a word even exists to describe our friendship. It is as though there is a thread that tethers us together. It loosens when we are apart, but grows taut when we are close.

I draw a fortifying breath before stepping into the night with my husband. I stay close by his side as we observe the destruction along the road. Two buildings have collapsed, and countless others are in shambles. People rush about, offering aid to their neighbors and combing through the damage. My breath catches at the catastrophic ruin of Saint Denis.

Odette should be here, helping our injured neighbors, not fleeing like a thief in the night. Laurence tightens his hold on my hand and tilts his head into mine. He plants a soft kiss on my cheek, lingering there as he whispers against my skin, "I am sorry, Cat. We must go."

"We have an hour, mon amour. How can I leave these poor souls to fend for themselves? They need Odette." I keep my voice low in the midst of the chaos and devastation around us.

The rough pad of his thumb strokes my cheek. His eyes are pained, dark, and desperately pleading for me to flee. "If the injured seek shelter in the cathedral, she may attend to them there if there is time."

A commotion sounds to our left. Royal soldiers are dispersing the crowd. My face heats as I watch soldiers forcing injured citizens away from the wreckage they have wrought.

A man with blood dripping from his hairline argues with a soldier. His hardened face is streaked with dirt, his clothes torn and disheveled. I cannot hear his words clearly, but he frantically points to the collapsed building before him. The soldier hits him with the butt of his rifle, and he collapses to the ground, unconscious from the vicious blow. Another soldier fires a shot into the crowd, causing a wave of bodies to fall to their knees while others scatter, searching for safe cover. I nearly jump out of my skin as the boom radiates in my chest.

To my surprise, the crowd begins to fight back, hollering and shoving at the soldiers and throwing bricks and other debris from the rubble strewn about the street.

"Cat! We *must* go." Laurence urges me in the direction of the cathedral.

We walk swiftly, weaving around obstacles and people huddled together amongst the wreckage. Laurie's satchel is brimming with evidence of our rebel activities. Our lives and the lives of our friends are at stake. We will be executed without a moment's hesitation if we are captured.

Shots continue to ring out, cutting through the pained wails and desperate pleas of the people we pass as they beg for our help. I avert my eyes from the children covered in blood and filth, much as it spears my heart to leave them here, injured and frightened. I must hold myself together and focus on our next destination so we may plan our counterattack and prevent this destruction from happening again.

My hand aches in Laurence's firm grip, but I do not let go. I walk as quickly as my legs will carry me, trying to keep pace with his longer strides. I understand his urgency; we must not be found out.

Finally, we climb the cathedral stairs. Mercifully, the Royal Army saw fit not to inflict its wrath upon this holy place— at least not yet. The church has been under the Royal Army's scrutiny for some time, executing des nonnes, the nuns of the Catholic church, as traitors for their unwillingness to pledge their loyalty to the state.

We must not linger a moment longer than necessary.

Throngs of people mill about on the street and stairs, some carrying travel bags, some donning their nightdresses, with shawls wrapped around their shoulders to shield them from the chill of the night air. Men and women carry crying children. All bear the look of quiet desperation—eyes dark with fatigue, bodies hunched as they shuffle up the stairs in search of asylum.

The doors are wide open, welcoming the victims of this monstrosity. Nonnes and enfants de chœur usher people to pews, handing out blankets and offering food and water. Two of the nuns are tending to the wounded.

My husband and I press on. We easily blend in with the masses and make our way to the front of the crossing, then disappear into a darkened corner in search of the stairs to take us to the lower level.

Laurence and I finally come upon our escape route, winding down the stone staircase into the bowels of the cathedral with torchlight on the walls to guide our way. As we complete our descent, we are consumed by the dark. Rushing water roars around us.

"Laurie?" I call out as I realize he has let go of my hand, my voice but a faint echo among the swell of the current running through the underground sewer system. I cover my nose with my hand and cough. The tunnel reeks with the unbearable stench of human waste and mold. I hope the others will be along quickly.

"I am here." Torchlight moves down the stairwell, illuminating our surroundings in its soft, orange glow. My husband appears, his long face pinched with disgust, brown eyes alight from the flame. I cannot help but laugh at his expression.

"I must say, mon amour, if you wished to whisk me away to be alone, I would prefer a more romantic locale." My nose wrinkles of its own accord as I dab the corners of my eyes with a handkerchief. "The accommodations leave much to be desired."

He sweeps me into his side with his free arm and kisses me, sending heat through my body despite our precarious situation. "My beautiful wife, when this is through, I vow to spend weeks locked away with you, tasting every inch of your body and drinking champagne." Laurence's teeth nip playfully at my bottom lip, and my cheeks flush at his words, but I lean into him, eager to feel his touch and to forget the unbearable circumstances of our lives for just a moment.

"I shall hold you to that promise," I say against his lips, unable to contain my coy smile as his fingers twist a lock of my hair.

For these few precious seconds, we allow the devastation around us to fall away, and we are the only two people in the world. Even in this horrible place, Laurence finds a way to remind me that he is my home, and I am his.

Hushed voices approach from the stairs, and we separate. Laurence steps in front of me, his large frame shielding me from whoever comes our way. I hold my breath, but feel my husband exhale at the same moment as we recognize Tomas' voice.

Tomas rounds the corner, torch in hand, with Jacquette and Claude huddled close behind. Jacquette's eyes shine with tears, and she covers her mouth, hiccupping on the stench. "Tomas, is this truly the best route to your home?" She buries her face in Claude's chest. "This is horrid!" Her voice is muffled as her husband pulls her closer.

"Je suis désolé, ma chère. I will buy you all the perfume you wish from Marie Catherine." Claude hugs his wife and turns to Tomas. "Tomas, how long will we be down here?"

Tomas laughs lightly, his hazel eyes crinkling at the corners. "Come now, Claude! We're having an adventure! Where is your sense of—" his words cut off by a coughing fit. Claude smacks him on the back a few times.

The disgusting combination of the smell and sheer dampness of this place is starting to make my head feel light and my stomach sour. "Tomas, I shudder to think what type of adventures you favor if this is where you have chosen to spend your time," I tease as he reaches us. "Dare I ask how you know the path to your home from here?"

"A man must have his secrets, Cat. It adds to my mystery. The ladies at the tavern find me whimsical, yet dangerous." Tomas winks, shadows playing across his face in the glow of his torch.

Everyone laughs and shakes their heads.

I groan at Tomas's attempt at levity, though I am still on edge and anxious for Odette's arrival. I can only imagine the situation on the streets has grown more precarious as the minutes tick by. This conflict is reaching its tipping point.

I can feel it in the air: the foreboding shadow of Death looms near, and we cannot escape him. We understand the risk of our actions. We understand the consequences, though we dare not breathe life into these thoughts with words.

My stomach clenches with distress at the thought of losing these people who have become my brothers and sisters. As quickly as the panic seizes me, it is gone, stolen away by the familiar tug I have come to recognize as Odette. The oddly shaped scar upon my chest, from which my Laurie named me, mon étoile, prickles, and I feel an inexplicable pull in the direction of the stairs.

She is here.

Olivier appears first, followed by my best friend, with Gerard close behind. Their hands grope at the wall beside them as they find their way through without a torch. Upon seeing me, Odette rushes to my side, and I catch her in my open arms. Relief runs through my veins, like a rushing river, to see her unharmed. The empty piece of my heart is filled once more by this woman who brings to life the most audacious pieces of myself without judgment.

"You are safe!" I say, fighting to hold back my tears. "I was so worried."

Odette's hold on me tightens. "It was awful. The people have taken to the streets. Riots are breaking out."

Gerard's booming voice calls for our attention. Odette and I pull apart, but she remains by my side, our arms linked together. "My brothers and sisters, the situation on Saint-Denis grows more dangerous by the minute. We must make haste. It is only a matter of time before the Royal Army breaches the cathedral. We must not be here when they arrive. Tomas, take the lead. We move out now."

Laurie whispers in my ear. "It is time to go, my star. Stay close to my side. Odette will be right here with us." I nod, hesitant to part from my friend, but I know our husbands only want to protect us. I kiss Odette's cheeks. "Let us leave this place. We will gorge ourselves with pastries and café tomorrow at my home."

"I shall hold you to that, ma chou." With a parting smile for my husband, Odette falls in step with Olivier as we descend further into the sewers with Tomas at the head of the line.

An hour later, we finally emerged onto the street above, tired and soaked in Paris's filth. When we arrive at Tomas's home, I cannot shed these cursed clothes and shoes quickly enough. My feet are freezing and chilled to the bone. After we are changed into dry clothes, we huddle around the hearth, covered in blankets. I sit between Laurie's legs and sink into his warmth with my back to his chest. For what feels like the first time in hours, I allow myself to exhale. His hands move up and down my arms, willing heat into my body.

Everyone and everything that matters to me in this world is huddled around me. I catch Odette's eye. The room is painted in the amber embrace of the fire, but not Odette— she exists in a halo of verte, like the leaves sprouting from trees in the spring. Her aura is life and rebirth, the world renewed. The pull in my chest is a comfort, knowing that mon sœur, my sister, in this life is near and is well.

She smiles weakly, and her eyes flutter shut, losing her battle with the exhaustion we all surely feel. Olivier cradles her, pressing his forehead to hers. The light from the fire casts a bronze glow across his deep brown cheeks. He kisses her gently on her nose, and I can practically feel Odette's stress melt away in the arms of her love.

While my body begs for sleep, my mind refuses to calm. The battle was too close tonight. We could have lost everything.

We could have lost each other.

Luck was on our side, but will our luck run dry? For how long can we outrun fate?

"Marie Catherine," Laurie whispers. "Quiet that brilliant mind of yours." My body is taut with apprehension as his arms swaddle me. "Breathe out, Cat. We are safe. I will never allow harm to come to you."

How does he not understand that it is not myself I fear for? I appreciate his steadfast commitment to me, but this is more than just my own life. "You cannot promise such things. And what of you? What of everyone in this room?"

Laurence's hand finds my cheek and tilts my face back toward his own. His soft lips press into my forehead, and he lingers for a moment, the rough pad of his thumb stroking my cheek. "Cat, sleep, my love. We will not solve this tonight. Let us be grateful for now. We live to fight another day."

All I can do is nod. I shift my position to sit across his lap and rest my head on his shoulder. He cradles me and is soon snoring softly, his breath tickling my face. The crackle and pop of the fire, with the heady smell of wood, offer a modicum of comfort. The hushed conversations around the room eventually die down, turning from murmurs to steady breaths and garbled snores.

My heartbeat gradually slows and falls into step with Laurence's, and I finally give in to my body's demand for sleep.

SCENE TWO

PARIS

TWO DAYS HAVE PASSED since the attack on Rue Saint-Denis. We returned today to offer our aid. The men are working tirelessly to help clear rubble and repair homes and businesses, and I join Odette at the Cathedral, tending to the injured. Jacquette is with us, distributing breads, cheeses, and fruits to those seeking refuge in the wake of the destruction of their homes.

Laurie and I closed Brume de Lavande yesterday to allow me time to focus on creating salves, poultices, and other remedies for Odette's patients. I created them using the old world methods of guérison de la terre, magic of the earth, sealing the medicines with enchantment for accelerated healing, good fortune, and protection.

They are, indeed, special.

The cathedral remains a temporary hospital for the most gravely injured. I walk the pews with Odette, offering my assistance and carefully following her instructions when she requires an additional set of hands. The pained moans and creaking of wood as the injured shift about uncomfortably echo through the sanctuary.

We approach a small girl; she must be no more than five years old. Her face is badly bruised, the shade of a plum. Blood crusts her hairline, and one eye is swollen shut. I bite down on my gasp and put on a brave face for her and her mother. Her mother wears the look of a woman who has crawled through the gates of Hell. She holds her daughter to her, making placating shushing sounds as the young girl cries with discomfort. Odette kneels before them, taking the child's tiny hand in her own. "Ma petite. Je m'appelle Odette. Je suis infirmière. Comment tu t'appelles?"

"Satine." Her voice is hushed through her tears.

"Such a beautiful name for a beautiful girl, Satine. And the bravest I have ever seen!" Odette turns to me, and I know she will want a healing salve for Satine's injury. I am ready with one of my best, charmed to alleviate the pain, and rolls of bandages. Odette's distress radiates through me. I place the supplies in her hand and cover them with my own, grounding her in the moment so she can perform her task.

"Merci." She smiles weakly, then straightens and gently cleanses Satine's wounds. Odette finishes and gently touches a finger to the girl's nose. Satine wrinkles her nose and smiles before burying her head in her mother's breast. My friend quietly explains to the mother how to care for the wound before moving down the line to the next patient.

I pause before following and pull a cherry candy from my skirt pocket and make a soft, whistling noise through my lips to attract Satine's attention. She peers at me with her uninjured eye, and I slip the sweet into her small hand, wink, and squeeze the mother's shoulder before following Odette.

Odette's usual green aura is tainted by a haze of black. Her eyes are soft and brimming with kindness, but the set of her jaw is tense as she works to set the broken arm of a young man. Beads of perspiration shimmer upon her brow.

"Cat, can you please help me hold his arm still while I wrap the splint?" I set down my bag and kneel next to her patient.

"See how I am holding his arm here?" I nod in response, furrowing my brow in concentration. "I am going to move one hand at a time. Replace my hands with your own in the exact places. Be firm, but do not apply pressure." I take a deep breath, intent on doing my duty well.

As Odette removes her hands, I slide my own into place as seamlessly as possible.

The patient hisses through his teeth, body tensing at the slight jostle. "Je suis désolé," I apologize, my heart aching at the pained expression on his face. He must be at least sixteen or seventeen, but the freckles scattered across his nose give him the appearance of a much younger boy. His eyes are glassy with tears, teeth clenched so hard I fear they will crack under the pressure.

"What is your name, monsieur?" I ask, wanting to help distract him from the pain and allow Odette to give her full attention to wrapping his arm.

"Martin," he responds, voice strained as Odette sets the splint against his forearm.

"I am Marie Catherine. Can you take a deep breath with me, Martin?" I catch his eye and hold it. He stares back and nods slowly. My lips curve slightly as I attempt to help this young man through the procedure. I inhale deeply through my nose and hold it, never breaking my stare, and Martin mimics the inhalation. I silently count to five, then blow the air through my mouth. He does the same.

"Let's do it again." We repeat the breathing three more times, as I help Odette, moving my hands at her command. I observe the moment the tension in his shoulders melts away, and feel Odette's stress dissipating at the same time. My scar pulses happily, like a kitten purring on my chest.

My friend wipes her chestnut hair from where it clings to her brow, damp with perspiration. "You did well, Martin. You must keep your arm splinted for three weeks. Do you live in the neighborhood?"

"Oui, madame."

"I shall return here three weeks from today to check on your arm. Can you meet me here after the morning service?"

"Oui. Merci. Merci, Marie Catherine."

"My friends call me Cat."

His nose scrunches at the familiarity of my name. "Are we to be friends?"

I chuckle and lightly squeeze his shoulder. "Martin, I have held your bones together. What more to friendship is there?"

SCENE THREE

PARIS

LONG HOURS PASS, AND Odette and I are dead on our feet. The setting sun outside gleams through the stained glass, casting a kaleidoscope of light across the sanctuary in a rainbow of colors. But we keep going. As long as there are patients in need, Odette will persist. Word spread throughout the neighborhood, drawing others to the cathedral in search of care or medicine. I handed out most of my stock hours ago, reserving what Odette needed to treat wounds.

Unfortunately, Laurence and I cannot afford to close the parfumerie for another day. I will need to spend the evenings creating more medicines and potions. The charms take careful concentration, but I will do whatever is necessary to ensure my friend has what she needs to heal her patients.

Odette is treating an elderly woman with a cough when she stumbles. I catch her arm, preventing her from falling. "Odette! Come, sit." I guide her to sit in the pew next to the woman. Her complexion has paled, and her hairline is soaked in sweat. Dark circles ring her eyes. She leans back, placing a hand to her forehead, and I fish a sweet from my pocket. "Here, eat this."

She attempts to wave me off. "Odette," I say sternly, my voice laced with warning. She has pushed herself for too many hours, and I cannot recall when we last ate or even had a sip of water. She reluctantly unwraps the cherry candy and crunches it between her teeth. "Stay here. I will find you some water."

"Oh, Cat. Please. I am fine. Just a little tired." Her tone lacks its usual vigor and command, but despite her protestation, she does not move from her seat.

"Excuse me, madame," I say to the woman. "Odette is through seeing patients today. If you mix licorice, vinegar, and oil, it will treat your cough. Take just a spoonful three times per day. We will return next week with more remedies." She nods her understanding and takes Odette's hand in her own, patting it a gentle, motherly way while I fetch water. I bring back two cups, one for each of them.

The woman shakes her head, sending her grey curls bouncing lightly. "Mon chou, drink." She gives her cup to Odette, holding it to her lips. "Go on."

"Madame, your cough…"

"Non. Drink. You are no use to us if you do not care for yourself." She turns her head and coughs into her shoulder. It is rough and rattles in her chest. I wince at the strength of the cough, knowing I will need to return soon with stronger medicine for her. I commit her house number and street to my memory, promising to see her in a day or two. There is nothing else Odette can do for her.

The woman offers her gratitude and shuffles away.

I take her seat, and Odette sinks into my side, her head falling to my shoulder. "Not a word, Cat." Some of her playfulness has returned.

I lay my head on hers. "I said nothing!"

She sighs. "I know your thoughts, Marie Catherine. I will have none of your impertinence tonight."

I stick another sweet in her face. "Even for another candy?"

She swipes it from my hand. "You will need to give me a wagon full of candies to tolerate your nonsense right now."

I can feel her smile. I kiss the top of her head and nuzzle into her hair. "I have nothing more to say that Madame Bernard did not say before she departed." Odette sighs with relief. "However," I continue, and she groans. "She is correct. I know you want to help as many people as you can, but you cannot help everyone. We should have left hours ago. You are only one woman, Odette."

"How can we leave all of these people?" She drops her voice to a whisper. "Cat, this will happen again. It may be worse."

"Then we must bring other doctors and nurses to our cause. You are not the only nurse in Paris. We will find a way."

My star warms on my chest. She is relaxed, and as much as I do not want to move Odette, we must leave. We need food, warm baths, and rest. I feel as though I could sleep for a week, but there is no time. There is never enough time.

I nudge Odette's side. "Let's find our husbands. They can fetch us a carriage home and rub our sore feet by the fire."

"What I desire is a very large goblet of wine." Odette rests her hands on her knees and pushes up to stand, stretching out her back as she does. "These pews were not meant to sit on all day. My backside aches something fierce."

"Then Olivier can rub your backside." A wicked grin crosses my lips, and I raise my eyebrows suggestively.

Odette looks positively scandalized, her round cheeks flushing pink. She swats at me with the back of her hand. "Hush, Cat. We are in the house of God."

I take her hand and guide her toward the door. "Then we must pray to God that Olivier takes great care of your aching backside."

"You are truly a wicked thing, Marie Catherine." My friend chastises me, but she is smiling and shaking her head at my brazenness, and that is all that I can ask for after this long day.

SCENE FOUR

PARIS

WE WALK HAND IN hand through the twilight. Despite the destruction, the evening is peaceful and still. Shops are shuttered, their lights extinguished for the night. People have returned to their homes, escaping the evening chill.

We find our husbands two streets away, gathered at a tavern with other members of the cause. They sit huddled in a back booth with tankards of ale. If one was unaware of the state of Rue Saint-Denis, the scene in the tavern appeared quite jovial. Groups of friends gathered for food and drink at the end of a hard day of work.

But as we approach the men, the spell is broken. Their faces are weary, their clothes covered in dirt and soot from clearing demolished buildings. Laurence gingerly grips his tankard as his knuckles are split with cuts. His eyes are dull and ringed with grey. I know that I must appear the same as our eyes meet. He glances between Odette and I, concern crinkling between his eyes.

Tomas stands and allows us to sit in the booth across from Olivier and Laurence, pulling up a chair from a nearby table for himself. A plate of picked-over bread and cheese sits in the middle of our table. My mouth practically waters just being in its presence. As though she can hear my thoughts, or perhaps the rumbling of my stomach, the barmaid arrives.

"Wine and two bowls of stew for the ladies," Laurence requests before the young woman can even ask if we need anything.

"Of course, monsieur. Another round for the table?"

"Oui. Merci." Laurence nods his thanks, and she disappears to the kitchen to our right. When the barmaid is out of sight, he leans across the table toward me. "We were beginning to worry, mon étoile. We were going to come search for you if you had taken much longer."

I shrug out of my cloak, and Odette speaks up beside me. "I apologize for keeping Cat for so long, Laurence. Word spread like wildfire that we were seeing patients, and well… as you can imagine, they flocked to us like locusts."

Laurence pins Odette with a serious stare. "Odette, you have nothing to apologize for. You and Cat are important to the cause. Your services were needed. That is that." Odette sits a little taller and touches a hand to her heart, and I wonder if she feels the same prideful flutter that radiates through my own chest.

Olivier beams across from Odette, eyes shining bright and wide at his wife. "You are magnificent, mon amour. We shall erect statues in your honor. Odette Bellamy, the Savior of Saint-Denis."

Her breath catches, and her cheeks burn as scarlet as the setting sun. "Olivier! You are ridiculous!"

Tomas's boisterous laugh shakes the table. He stands and takes a knee, bowing deeply to Odette. "Sainte Odette of Montemarte."

The barmaid returns just then with two steaming bowls of stew and crusty bread, her face screwed up in confusion, which only makes the entire table burst with laughter. "You must excuse Tomas," I tell her. "He is a bit touched. His maman dropped him right on his head as a babe." I lightly tap the side of my head and pout my lips. "The poor, dear."

The corners of her bow-shaped mouth turn downward. "Oh!" she exclaims, as Tomas cranes his neck and smiles up at her. I brace myself for whatever is to come from his mouth next, feeling sorry for this poor girl.

Tomas spins on a knee and takes one of her hands, planting his lips to her knuckles. "Ma chérie, you must not believe these uncultured heathens. They are overcome with jealousy of my wit and dashing looks."

She snatches her hand back and narrows her eyes at Tomas, appraising him coolly. "I know of you, Tomas Boucher. I hear your… affliction leaves women bored and wanting."

Her gaze lowers to below his belt, and my mouth gapes open like a cod fish. Laurie and Olivier do not even attempt to hide their glee. They are hunched over their drinks, howling with laughter.

Our embarrassed friend rises to his feet, straightens his shirt, and harumphs. "Some people just do not appreciate my superior charm. And I have *no* affliction!" With a sweeping flourish, Tomas throws on his jacket and walks briskly from the tavern with his head held high.

Olivier places a few coins on the table for the barmaid. "Merci, Louisa."

She takes the coins and pockets them in her skirts, winking at us. "I'll be back with your drinks in just a moment." I notice there is more confidence in her gait as she leaves us.

Odette is dabbing the corner of her eyes with the sleeve of her dress, still shaking with uncontrollable chuckles. For the first time in several days, I feel light and happily dig into my stew. The rich flavors of thyme and sage explode on my tongue and warm my belly as I swallow down a large bite. With no care for manners, I inhale my bowl, shoveling in large mouthfuls. Louisa hides a smile behind her hand when she comes back with ale for Laurence and Olivier. I am grateful for the wine and take a big gulp to wash down my bite of bread soaked in gravy.

I look up from my food to see my companions gawking at me. I feel a dribble of gravy run down my chin, which Laurie wipes with his thumb, clucking his tongue in quiet chastisement. "Mon étoile." He exhales through his nose, but he is smiling, and the shine in his eyes has finally returned. Warmth spreads through me, but it is no longer from the stew.

This man… how fortunate I am to be loved so completely by him.

After I practically inhale a second bowl, and Odette also finishes her meal, our husbands update us on the situation in the neighborhood. There are rumors of more attacks planned for other parts of the city in the days to come: Belleville, Montrogue, and La Villette.

Laurence and I live in an apartment above the parfumerie. It is tiny, just our bedroom, bathing chamber, and living area that includes our kitchen, but we do not require much. The most important feature of the shop is what lies below: our faction's headquarters.

Though the basement is somewhat cramped, we have enough room for provisions, weapons, and a small table for meetings. If necessary—if the unthinkable were to occur — we can offer shelter to roughly ten people. It would be tight, but more crucially, it would be safe.

The fighting should not reach our shop, but our friends may not be so lucky. They live in the working-class boroughs to the northeast of the city: the places most vulnerable and at risk of falling during an attack.

I suddenly feel cold, the sensation driving deep into my bones. Something doesn't feel quite right, but I cannot place the source of my unease. It is like the hand of Death is calling out, demanding recompense for lives owed. My head swims, and the room tilts and swirls around me. The revelry and merriment around us becomes but a pulsing din beyond the ringing in my ears. The room is blanketed in a veil of grey, like I am peering through a curtain. My hands grip the rough wood of the edge of the table before me until I feel like it could splinter from the force.

"Cat? *Cat?*" Hands grasp my shoulder, shaking me roughly. The world comes blazing back into focus, and I am met with Laurence's panic-stricken face. Odette's hand has a death-grip on my shoulder. I blink rapidly, trying to make sense of what just happened.

"Marie Catherine. What is wrong, mon étoile?"

I blink at my husband, trying to form a coherent response, but only come up with a shuddering breath. I place a hand to my forehead and find it slick with sweat.

"I suppose the drink and exhaustion are going to my head." I force a small smile, hoping to reassure him that I have not entirely lost my senses or fallen ill, though I don't quite believe either, myself.

Odette's hand finds my cheek. "Cat, you are so cold, but sweating. I think it's best we get you home. Olivier, can you please get a carriage for Laurence and Cat back to the city?"

Before Laurie or I can object, Olivier is out the door to the street beyond.

"Odette, really. I am fine." But I am not fine, and she will not be swayed by my objections.

"Marie Catherine Durand, you are leaving right this instant and going straight to your bed." I let her help me up from the booth, where she then turns me over to Laurence's open arms. He links an arm through my own, leaves payment on the table, then leads me out to the waiting carriage. Olivier closes the door behind us, and I sag into my seat.

"Take care, Cat. I will bring Odette tomorrow to check in on you."

"*Merci*, Olivier. *Bonne nuit*," I wish him goodnight.

As the carriage begins to move, Laurence tucks me into his side. I am asleep before we make it to the end of the road.

SCENE FIVE

PARIS

I AWAKEN IN THE early hours of dawn in my own bed. The sun has not yet greeted us with her amber kiss, but the sky outside is violet as the morning bids us hello. The hearth across the room is reduced to embers. I do not have the energy to place another log to rekindle the flame. Instead, I sink back into the blankets.

Laurence sleeps soundly next to me, an arm wrapped protectively around my waist. His body radiates the heat I seek. I move closer so my back is to his chest, curling into him. His arm tightens, and his breath tickles my ear. "Sleep, Cat," his husky voice gently commands.

But I cannot sleep. Physically, I feel better. The chill has passed, but my mind is overcome with a million thoughts and worries. What happened last night? I am not prone to premonition, but my grand-mère had the gift of sight. Would it be so unbelievable if I had developed the ability? It did not feel like a vision, exactly. It was more of an encroaching fear or a warning.

If I did, in fact, have a vision, it can only mean catastrophe is near. We cannot possibly continue to evade the Royal Army; they have spies everywhere. It is only a matter of time before our luck runs out.

It is only a matter of time before the darkness claims one of our own.

Fate will not be deterred by the whims of mere men.

"Oh, Cat." Laurie turns me to face him and brushes his hand to my cheek, smearing the tears that I had not realized were falling. My body is racked by sobs that steal my breath. "What troubles you, little star?"

"Something is going to happen, Laurie," I breathe. "I can feel it. Deep in my very soul, I feel it."

His brow furrows, and his eyes search mine for answers that I am unable to fully verbalize. "Feel what?"

My heart thunders against my chest as though it is trying to escape, and my chest heaves, a sob caught in my throat. I choke out the words that repeat over and over in my mind. "The end of everything."

His hand moves to the back of my head, winding through my hair and pulling me forward until his warm lips begin kissing away my tears. "My little star," he whispers against my cheek. "These are dark times, but we will endure. We will endure together. You will see. All will be well, and I will do as I promised and take you away from here. We will live a life of leisure in the countryside. We will drink wine, have horses and pigs, and a garden full of delicious vegetables, herbs, and flowers for your perfume and potions. Anything you want."

I laugh through my tears at the thought of my sweet Laurie, who has only known life in Paris, attempting to wrangle a pig.

"There she is. There is mon étoile. The light of my days and my nights."

Peering up at him through blurry eyes, I see the love and promise that he would never allow harm to befall me. Despite these difficult times we live in, I believe him. Or at least I believe he will try until his own dying breath. I push a lock of hair from his brow and stare deep into his eyes, feeling the connection between us. Something stirs in my belly—something hot and full of need.

"Laurie." His name is a plea that he answers without hesitation, capturing my mouth with his own and kissing me as though I am the very thing that breathes life into him.

The world around us falls away, and I lose myself in his touch. We shed our clothes in a flurry of passion and desperation. I luxuriate in the feel of his skin against my own, as his scent envelopes me. Teakwood and bergamot— masculine yet fresh and light.

The weight of Laurie on me is a comfort. My solace. My safety. My home.

I wrap my legs around him, pulling him closer. "Mon étoile." His husky voice in my ear sends shivers through me. He takes his time tracing his mouth down my jaw to my neck with purpose, knowing each place on my body that will make me moan and cry out his name. I gasp as he fills me, and I sink back into the bed, consumed by him.

"Je t'aime, mon amour," he professes his love.

My breath is ragged as he moves inside me, overwhelmed by the sensation of his hard length and his mouth kissing and nipping at my collarbone. "Mon cœur," I breathe. My heart. He is my heart.

The fighting, the hurt, the danger fade to the deepest recesses of my mind. For just today, only Laurence and I exist.

SCENE SIX

PARIS

MY BASKET IS BRIMMING with herbs, flowers, beeswax, oil, and pencils from the market. My stores for creating remedies are low, so I made sure to gather everything I need and more, just to be prepared. Odette walks beside me with her own basket of goods. Laurence is working the counter at the store today so that Odette and I can stow away in the apartment, replenishing medicines and salves. I wish to teach Odette charms.

She has power in her that she has not yet discovered. But I sense it. Like calls to like. I would recognize that energy as sure as the nose on my face. I know with time and some patience that I can coax her power forth.

Shielding my eyes against the sun's midday brilliance with my free hand, I turn to my friend, a question dancing upon my tongue. We have never spoken of the invisible thread that binds us, nor have we addressed my own relationship with the earth's energy. It never seemed necessary. We were drawn together from the start, and that was enough for us.

But I want more. In the absence of my maman and grand-mère, my soul is desperate for that connection. Charms are more powerful when bound by the energy of two.

Odette looks at peace in my company. It is time. "Odette?" Her name comes out as a question laced with uncertainty.

"What troubles you? Your face is scrunched like you are sorting an unsolvable riddle."

Hells and damnation. I did not mean to begin this conversation with such a troubled tone. I loosen the tension in my cheeks and lick my lips before beginning again. "Nothing is the matter. I only wish I had brought a parasol or worn a hat. The sun is trying to cook my face. I feel like a chicken roasting over the hearth."

Odette's giggle brings a smile to my face. "Oh, Cat. You are so dramatic. You may have been born for theater rather than perfume and medicine."

"I am not dramatic! I simply do not require additional sun when I am already the light of so many lives."

She links an arm through mine and kisses my cheek as we walk in the direction of my store. "I apologize, my dear shining star. However, when you do make your debut at the theater, I demand the best seats in a private box."

I scoff. "You make many demands for someone who is poking fun at my radiance."

"You are the most radiant woman I have ever known. Now, my shining star, what did you want to ask me?"

I'd almost forgotten that I had wanted to discuss her latent power in the wake of our jesting. "Oh, yes. This may sound odd, but I promise to explain everything. When we are together or even in close proximity, do you ever feel a sort of...pull in your chest?" I extract my arm from Odette's and rub at the spot on my chest where I bear my scar. As though it knows I am speaking of it, it thrums with happy energy, pleased to be in Odette's company. "Here, in this spot. Do you feel that?"

Odette sucks her lower lip into her mouth and narrows her eyes in concentration. I stop walking and move my hand to the center of her chest, right above her breasts. "Right here, Odette." We lock eyes, and her breath hitches for a moment at my touch, then her hand moves to mine and grasps it. She slowly nods, her eyes pooling with tears.

"It's you," she whispers. "You are my second heartbeat."

Heartbeat?

We stand still on the sidewalk as I allow her words to wash over me. A second heartbeat. Is that what I feel within my chest when Odette is near?

Is this the cause of the inexplicable ache within me when we are apart? When did the ache begin? Was it always there? I search my memory, but am filled with uncertainty.

She tugs on my hand, extricating me from my thoughts and prodding me to begin walking again. "Come, Cat. There is much we must discuss." She drops her voice. "But not here."

What does Odette know?

Excitement mixed with overwhelming relief courses through my body as we hurry to Brume de Lavande, our boots tapping a quick, joyous tune upon the cobblestones. It is all I can do to suppress the laugh bubbling up in my throat.

We rush into the shop, and the bell above the door greets us with its tinkling chime. Laurence appears from the back room holding a small box of perfume and places it on the counter. "Good afternoon, ladies. I would ask if you are having a pleasant afternoon, but you look like a cat who has caught a mouse."

Placing my basket of goods next to the box, I throw myself into his arms, and he catches me and spins me in a circle. "Marie Catherine, what has gotten into you today?" He kisses my brow, and his smile is wide.

"It is just a wonderful day!"

He kisses me again, this time on my lips. "I am glad." He sets me down and straightens his shirt, suddenly remembering that I did not arrive alone. He inclines his head. "Odette. How are you?"

"I am well, Laurence." She gestures with her basket. "Cat and I are going to replenish salves and remedies. We saw so many patients at the cathedral that we used everything."

Laurie hands me my basket. "Then I shall leave you, ladies, to your work and see you for supper."

We head into the back room and take the stairs to my apartment, locking ourselves away. When we are finally settled, our supplies neatly organized and laid out on the small wooden table in our main living area,

Odette speaks first. Her brown eyes are practically bursting with joy. "I need to show you something." She unbuttons her olive-colored muslin dress to her breast and pulls the fabric open. My heart stops, and my hands fly to my mouth, muffling the stunned cry.

How is this possible? How do two women bear the same oddly shaped scar? My fingers move absently to my own scar, Laurie's name for me echoing in my ears: mon étoile.

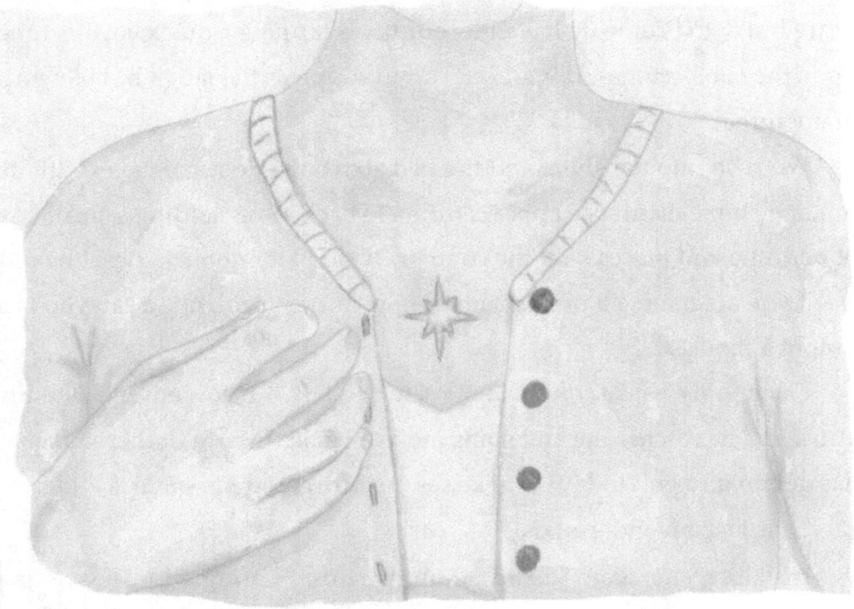

My heart is racing like a mare through a meadow. Odette's aura glows brilliant gold, enshrouding her like an ethereal being. I struggle to find my voice, but my friend waits patiently as I sort through the mix of emotions rolling through my body.

I stand from my chair and lean on the table, rooting myself in the moment. I allow my emotions to wash over me until I reach a point of clarity. When I look up from the table and meet Odette's eyes, a relieved laugh bubbles up my throat. "Odette. We're the same. How long have you known? Why did you not tell me?"

She smirks. "Ma chou, did you truly believe that I did not know your remedies are charmed? I recognize myself in you. Like calls to like. We are bound by the stars and the heavens."

My face falls with disbelief. "Odette! How could you keep this from me for so long?"

Aghast, she throws my words right back to me. "You are one to talk, Marie Catherine." Her full eyebrows rise to meet her hairline, playfully scolding me for my own sin of secrecy.

I cannot believe it. All this time, all these years, and I have a sister in the earth's magic once more. A practitioner without a coven is a lonely existence— our energy yearns for companionship. It begs of us to join our energy, to mold it and place it back into the universe.

I move around the table and kneel before my friend, my sister, and clasp one of her hands in mine. "Mon sœur. My sister. After all this time." Happy tears stream from my eyes. "After all this time, I have someone to share in this gift."

She flicks my freckled nose. "Ma chou, you have been my sister since the first day we met. Now then, get up. There is work that must be done."

Her words rejuvenate me. I retrieve my family grimoire from the shelf in the corner of the kitchen and flip through the pages in search of the charm for a salve that heals burns, when something prickles at the back of my mind. I cease turning the pages and listen to my body. A feeling passes through me, guiding me to a passage from my arrière grand-mère, one I have not thought of in years. I splay open the well-loved pages of the history of ma famille before Odette. The page is covered in Bonne-Maman Marguerite's elegant script.

"Do you see?" I enthusiastically thrust a finger at the page, forgetting myself and almost tearing the delicate parchment. Quickly, I pull back and clasp my hands behind my back.

As Odette's eyes search the text, the light surrounding her shimmers. Glancing up from the page, she tilts her head in askance, hair falling over an eye. "Do you believe this to be true?"

I nod my head so hard I feel lightheaded. "I do. I never paid the passage much mind, but this," I gesture between us, "is proof. Is it not?" Taking the book, I recite the notes.

A soul is not born for a solitary life. It requires nourishment, community, companionship, and adulation. A soul seeks its mirror, its mate. You will feel your mirror in the depths of your heart, beating like the wings of a sparrow. It calls out to you. For those with devotion to the stars, you may join your soul to its mirror. In this joining, you will never again find yourself without love.

Gingerly, I close the grimoire and hug it to my chest. It hums with auspicious energy, pleased to have served its bearer.

"It is you, Odette. You are my mirror."

Odette is upon me in an instant, folding me into her nurturing embrace. "And you are mine, Marie Catherine. You are mine."

We fall into our easy way of working together, but it is different now. More intimate as we share in our knowledge of earth magic and charms. Odette adds her own formulas and enchantments to the grimoire, binding us in a new way. A grimoire is sacred. It is no small thing, taboo even, to allow a practitioner from another family to contribute to your grimoire.

This is different. If Bonne-Maman speaks true, Odette is ma famille the same as the women who came before me. She is my sister, the same as if we had shared a womb. The fates and the stars forever entwine us.

And our magic... our magic is both fiery and delicate, imbuing our remedies with healing and good fortune for the body and the soul. I have never felt anything quite like our joined energy. There is harmony to it and breathtaking opalescent light.

The hours pass in the blink of an eye, the candles around us are burned down to nubs, when I hear the steady fall of Laurie's boots on the stairs. Engrossed in our work, supper was forgotten. Sheepishly, I smile at my husband. He simply shakes his head, no doubt unsurprised by my oversight, and hangs a pot over the hearth to prepare stew. There is a bit of bread left from our breakfast.

Collecting her half of the remedies into her basket, Odette bids us farewell, needing to return home to Olivier.

She has barely passed the threshold when the ache in my chest begins.

SCENE SEVEN

PARIS

DAYS PASS WITH RELATIVE peace. As promised, Odette and I return to Saint-Denis to check in on how her patients are faring while Laurie, Olivier, Tomas, and Gerard hold a meeting in our basement. While the week may have been peaceful, I am not foolish enough to fall into a false sense of security. We are in the midst of conflict. The winds can and will change without warning.

Martin's face lights up with glee when he enters the sanctuary, spotting me and Odette moving about the pews, distributing medicine and healing tea and tonics to those in need, and inspecting the progress of healing wounds. His arm is still splinted, but there is a lightness to him that was not there a week ago. I envy his youthful vigor.

It has not escaped my attention that he wears long pants, rather than knee breaches, which are much more common. Could he be a member of the sans-culottes, another rebel faction in our cause?

I am torn in this moment between wishing to recruit him into our assembly and wanting to protect him from the danger and cruelty of it all, if he is unattached in this fight. He is so young, but what will become of his life if this conflict continues to crush us under the weight of oppression? What future might he have if he were to join us and help us turn the tide?

There is no easy answer, but I would be remiss not to give him the choice. He walked away from the last attack with his life. Would he be so lucky when it comes again?

And so, I put a smile on my face and beckon the young man to us, waving a hand in the air.

"Marie— I mean, Cat. I am so pleased to see you."

I pull him into a gentle embrace. "Martin, you look well." And I mean it. His coloring has returned, his nose and cheeks pink with the kiss of sunshine, and his hair is neatly combed and tied back with a bit of leather. "Are you having any pain?" I riffle through my satchel in search of a pain tonic, but he waves me off with his good hand.

"It is tolerable. Please, save your medicine for someone who needs it more."

"Merci, Martin. Sit, Odette should be along in a moment." A few feet away, my sister is speaking softly with a pregnant woman. They appear quite occupied. An indecipherable voice whispers in my ear. I cannot distinguish the words; however, my intuition knows. Receiving messages from the universe does not require spoken language. My body is attuned to hear its call.

The message is clear: Martin is important.

Glancing around to ensure we may speak freely, I determine we shall not be overheard by prying ears. Odette has taken her patient from the sanctuary to examine her in private. Sliding down the pew closer to Martin, I drop my voice to just barely a whisper. "Martin, what are your thoughts on the monarch?"

"I…well…I um," he sputters, unable to find his words.

"It is just that I noticed how you dress, and I had wondered if perhaps you were *active* in some way?"

His brown eyes grow wide with shock, darting here and there with worry. "Cat, do you speak of…treason?" He whispers the last word.

My stomach plummets. "Non! Of course not." The words rush from my mouth. "Not of treason. Of—," I pause, my mind frantically searching for words that will not implicate Laurie and our friends in crimes against the crown. "I speak of *change*." I pin him with a penetrating stare, hoping to communicate my true meaning.

Martin leans in close. "Tell me. I wish to hear your thoughts."

Taking his hand, I slide across the pew so that we are but a breath away from one another. "Is it treasonous to wish for a better life, Martin? Is it treason to believe that our citizens should continue to live destitute and struggle to survive while others have excess? More food than can possibly fill their bellies? More beds in their homes than family members to occupy them, while children sleep on the street with no food and not a flame to keep them warm?

"I do not have much, Martin, but I have more than most. I have a place to lay my head, and I worry not where my next meal comes from. I wish to live in a world where we all have the necessities that allow us to flourish. To be *free*."

My chest shudders as I exhale, trying with all my might not to cry. We sit together, silent, staring into one another's eyes— mine pleading, his questioning as he considers my words. His aura is grey as slate, eyes teeming with fear and uncertainty.

The suspense is more than I can bear, my heart thundering against my chest with apprehension that I misunderstood the message. Martin, fortunately, does not make me wait long for his answer. "I do not believe your ideals are treason, Cat. But the monarch does. I am one man. Papa has gone to God. I care for my mother and sister, and we are just scraping by. I cannot work in the factory with my injury. We have but perhaps a day's more food before it runs out." His head hangs in shame. I feel melancholy and desperation in him. It is heartbreaking. Consuming.

Tentatively, I cup his chin and raise his face until he sits straight and tall. "Join us, Martin. Let us fight for a better life for us all."

SCENE EIGHT

PARIS

OUR BASEMENT IS PALPABLE with determined energy. Claude's spy within the Royal Army delivered news this afternoon. Our men are congratulating Claude, clapping him on the back and cheering for his success. The tide may finally turn in our favor. Gerard stands on a chair in the middle of the small space and holds up his hand, signaling for silence.

I huddle against a wall with Odette and Jacquette, quietly taking in the meeting. Martin sits among the men, observing his unfamiliar surroundings. He does not seem nervous, although he looks like a child among our husbands and friends. He sits tall and proud, though, eager to change his station. Young men like Martin inspire hope, and hope starts with a ripple. Martin and his friends can help create waves that will reshape France's future.

Gerard's booming voice calls my attention. "Frères et sœurs. Mes amis. Ma famille. The fight of our lives is upon us. Liberty is within our grasp." Gerard closes his hand into a fist and pauses, looking us each in the eye. "What shall liberty bring? We do not fight for abundance. We do not fight for extravagance while our brothers and sisters suffer, living off the meager crumbs the monarchy feels we are deserving of. We deserve to do more than survive. We deserve to live. To earn a living wage so that we may fill our bellies and raise our families in comfort."

We cheer in response, and the men pound their fists on the table in a steady rhythm. Martin is swept up in the excitement, pounding his fist with a brilliant smile across his lips. Laurie claps him on the shoulder and shakes him a few times, joy radiating from him.

"Paris does not belong to the Crown! It belongs to the people," Gerard continues from atop his chair. "Claude brings us news of the Army's plans. An attack is coming in three days time." Climbing down from his chair, our leader paces to the wall where maps hang and begins detailing the Royal Army's plans.

The world around me begins to fade, and the voices of my loved ones feel far away.

It is happening again.

Dread courses through my veins like an icy river, chilling me to the bone. My limbs tremble so much that it is as though the floor has dropped from beneath my feet. Not wanting to cause a scene or worry Laurie, I move to lean into Odette, but she is already there, gathering me in her arms and escorting me from the room that suddenly feels claustrophobic, whispering to Olivier on the way out that we are headed outside for some fresh air.

We do not go outdoors. She escorts me directly to my apartment and helps me to my bed so that she may fetch some water. I squeeze my eyes shut, trying to will my head to cease its incessant pounding and to make the room stop spinning like a whirlpool around me. Cool cloth meets my forehead as Odette dabs a damp handkerchief to my face.

"Lie still, ma petite chou. I'll return in a moment." She situates the cloth across my forehead and leaves the room. Her absence is a tiny hole in my heart that grows wider with each step she takes away from me.

Raw emotion pushes and pulls in different directions, contending for space within my body. This time is worse than before. Death doesn't just chase us; Death will claim one among us. I cannot breathe for the unbearable weight of this revelation sits nestled in my chest, smothering in its force.

I feel Odette before I see her. The pressure in my breast loosens its hold slightly. "Sit up. Drink." She slides a hand under my neck and holds my head up just enough that I may drink from the cup. The spice and smoke of whiskey infiltrate my nose, followed by the sharp burn of the dark liquid in my throat. "Slowly, now. I'm not meaning to make you drunk, just to settle your nerves a bit." The mug disappears from my lips, and she gently lowers my head back to the pillow. The mattress shifts slightly with her weight. Sitting next to me, Odette tenderly brushes my hair from my face.

"How lucky I am to have a nurse as my best friend," I jest, trying to erase the worry between her brows, but to no avail.

"What has happened? The pain and agitation within you is like an inferno. Where does this come from?"

A thump forms in my throat, threatening to choke me, but I must tell Odette. I must warn her of this premonition of disaster, of death. Perhaps I can convince her to flee this place. My heart cannot bear to lose the family that I have only just claimed as my own.

I swallow thickly around the lump in my throat. "I do not know for certain. I do not know what is to happen, only that it will be soon. There will be loss. Unimaginable loss. I cannot say who, but Death has arrived, and he will make his claim, my sweet Odette."

I sit up, panic seizing me, and grab hold of her face. Her eyes are full of terror, but the words spill from me quickly and with desperation. "Please. You must leave Paris. You and Olivier. I cannot bear to lose you, Odette. The pain would be too great. I beg of you, to flee tonight, before it is too late." A sob escapes my aching throat.

"And where will you be? What of you?"

My eyes flutter closed, and I focus on the message the All Mother and the universe is trying to convey to me. What is my role? Where am I meant to be?

Opening my senses and clearing my mind, I isolate myself from outside forces, including the beating of Odette's heart in time with my own. Faintly, I hear a murmur among the noise. It is low, but consistent, repeating its edict. I know what I must do, though it pains me so.

Odette's expression falls before the words cross my lips. "My place is here. I cannot leave. I am meant to be here."

"Then this is where I am meant to be as well." Her hand raises to cut off my protestation. "Cat, I will hear no further debate on the topic. If the unthinkable is to occur, then my place is here where I can be of service."

I should know better than to attempt to sway Odette. She is steadfast, immovable. Through my tears, I nod. "Then we do this together."

Her fingers tilt my chin up ever so slightly. "With confidence, mon chou," she instructs.

My shoulders roll down my back, and my head lifts, determination burning within our shared hearts. "We do this together."

Her brown eyes crinkle, pleased with my compliance. "Good."

SCENE NINE

FRANCE

THE MORNING IS QUIET. Laurence and I clean and restock the store's shelves in companionable silence, neither of us wanting to sour the mood with talk of the battle to come. If Claude's report is correct, the Royal Army will infiltrate the Faubourg Saint-Antoine neighborhood in two days. But we will be ready to defend our sans-culottes friends in the lower districts.

Libelle were distributed throughout the neighborhood in secret, warning of the attack and calling our community to stand with us. The response was so great that our meeting last night had to be moved to another location. Tomas found the Madame of a brothel who was more than willing to accommodate, allowing use of the attic.

The plans are set in motion. Our men will launch a surprise attack on the Army tomorrow, when we anticipate they will move in to set up their barricade.

I cannot dispel the ache in my chest, but I continue my work, hoping to lose myself in the motion of my day. Laurie's familiar scent wraps me in its cocoon. His hands rest at my hips, and I drop my rag, surprised by his touch as I was consumed with cleaning a shelf. "You are so quiet." He spins me to face him. His handsome face is pinched with worry. He trails a knuckle along my jaw, and I lean into his touch, craving it. "Tell me. What is that brilliant mind thinking?"

Sighing, I lean back against the wall. "What do you think of Tomas and Gerard's plan? Speak plainly, mon amour. Please."

He runs a hand through his hair and lowers his head, and it is all the answer I need. "It is the only plan we have. There is no better option that I can see. We must act on Claude's report. If we do not, I fear we will lose everything."

"But what if his report is false? What if his spy is wrong? What if he is deceiving us? Is it not possible that this man is using Claude?" I exhale, shaking my head. "I am sorry, my love. I do not mean to question our friends, but I still have this terrible feeling. I trust my intuition more than the words of a member of the very army that means to lead us to the gallows."

"All of those things may very well be true, Cat. But we must do something. To do nothing would be to our detriment. We must act."

I know he is right, and the one man I do trust with my whole being is Laurie. If he saw another way, he would make his voice heard. This may not be the best plan, but we are out of options, and we are out of time. Sighing in resignation, I move into Laurie, wrapping my arms around him.

He returns my hug. "All will be well, you'll see. We have each other. They cannot take that from us."

I smile into his chest, inhaling his teakwood and bergamot scent into my lungs. He is my guiding light in the darkness. "I love you, Laurie."

His chin rests atop my head. "My shining little star. I love you. We shall endure."

The bell above the shop door tinkles, announcing our first customer of the morning. Laurie steals a quick kiss before turning to greet our patron, and I bend to grab my rag and return to my cleaning.

"Bonjour, monsieur. How may I help you? What are you—? No!"

There is a flurry of activity behind me, and I quickly turn to see what has happened when a concussive sound pierces the quiet of our morning. My ears ring with a high-pitched whine. Smoke obscures my vision. Laurie! Where is Laurie?

I see him by the counter, screaming with primal rage, slamming his fist into the man who had just entered our shop over and over.

I stumble forward, blinded by searing pain followed by the crack of my knees hitting the wood floor. The intruder's body drops beside me, unmoving.

"Cat! No, Cat!" Laurie's frantic cries are muffled as he kneels beside me. My head is light. I cannot stop myself from falling the rest of the way to the floor, though my husband's hands catch me. His face swirls above me, and nausea rises in my throat. I close my eyes, trying to block out the chaos unleashed around me.

All that exists is the intense fire raging in my abdomen.

"No, no, no. Open your eyes, little star. Look at me." His rough hands pat my cheek. I crack open an eye to find my vision has cleared slightly. The smell of gunpowder has overtaken the tranquil fragrances of my parfumerie. I try to sit up, a shriek ripping from my throat at the agonizing pain. I grab at my belly, finding it slick to the touch.

I raise a shaking hand and find it dripping bright crimson.

Laurie is frantic, tearing off his shirt. "You're going to be fine." His voice trembles, giving away what I already know. He holds the torn garment to my abdomen, and I writhe, crying out. "I'm sorry, Cat. I must staunch the bleeding. I promise, you will be fine. Hold this here. I must fetch Odette, and she will heal you. You'll be good as new, you'll see." He takes my hand and pushes on it to apply pressure to my wound.

I scream again at the burning pain radiating through my ravaged belly. "No! Do not leave me. *Please.* Laurie, do not go!"

Odette is already on her way. Despite everything, I can feel her. My scar prickles, the sensation intensifying each moment as she makes her way to me. The beat of her racing heart pumps in time with my own.

Laurence, my sweet husband, is overcome with hiccuping sobs. "I have to go, Cat. I must get help. You are so strong. Burn bright, my star. I'm getting help." His shaking lips press to mine. "I love you, Marie Catherine. I *will* return." He picks up the abandoned pistol from beside the unconscious man. Shots ring out outside in a steady barrage of booms, mixed with shouts and breaking glass.

Death's cool hand strokes my face. It is gentle, prodding me to whatever comes next. But Laurence...

No. It cannot be his time, too.

Please, just me. Just take me.

"Please, Laurie! I beg of you, do not go!"

But he is already running to the door. He turns to spare me one last glance when my world goes red. The window pane in our door shatters, and all I can do is scream as my husband's head violently snaps backward and his body crashes to the ground.

With all of my strength, I roll to my belly, still clutching his shirt to my wound with one hand. I try to crawl to him, inching on one elbow and pushing my feet to propel me forward. "Laurie! No!" My body is wracked with sobs as it gives out under my own weight. I cannot make it to him. But it does not matter.

He is unmoving, blood pooling around his head.

With a roar, I attempt to push myself once more toward my husband, but I fail, collapsing as my arm gives out. Choking, the taste of copper fills my mouth, and my blood splatters as I cough roughly, face down on the floor.

Odette. She is near. But she will be too late. I can feel her running for me, her mind calling out to my own. But it is not my name she calls.

Chiara.

An Italian name. A beautiful name.

I lay with my cheek to the rough, wooden floor, tears crashing over me in waves of despair. My sweet Laurie. All I want is to breathe my final breath next to him. I want one last moment to touch him before we move to our next life together.

Hold on, Chiara. I'm coming for you.

Glass spills across the shop floor, followed by an amber glow.

I am so cold.

Stay with me, Chiara.

The name is so familiar. Why do I know it?

Heat kisses my face, but it does not warm me. Sleep. What if I just sleep?

"Chiara! Oh no. No! Laurence."

Laurence.

My husband.

My love.

My light who shines no more.

My chest shudders with cries that are too painful to let go of.

Odette's beautiful golden halo is all around me. She came. Her heart beats strong in my chest, but it is not enough as my own fades to a whisper.

Gently, she rolls me to my back, gasping at my ruined abdomen. "No," she breathes. "Oh, my sister. No. Not again." She pulls my head into her lap and strokes my hair. Her tears caress my cheeks like a gentle rain shower. "Can you stand? We need to get out of here. The fire…We have to move, now."

Fire. I remember fire.

I remember…

My body seizes as memories of another lifetime flash through my mind. Illness and despair. A dear friend who understood the same loss I experienced. A cottage filled with magic. Wine and late nights laughing by the hearth. A life reborn from the ashes of grief, only to be burned again by hate. A warm, summer day beneath a weeping willow. The bow of a boat destined for France.

She fought for us. She fought for me.

And she is here again in this life to fight for me again.

My voice is soft when I finally speak her name: the name of the person I bound to me throughout the ages, all those years ago in a tiny cottage because I refused to live a single life without her. "Marcella."

She hiccups on a sob as she hears her true name for the first time in over one hundred years. "Thank the All Mother. You remember."

My head is so heavy. "I could never forget."

"No, you are too stubborn for that. Now, my stubborn sister, we need to leave. We don't have much time."

No. We do not. My time is at an end. Death will not continue to wait.

"Marcella, my time is done. You must go." I cannot control the cough that comes rattling from my chest.

"Oh, Chiara. No! I will not lose you. Not again!" The fury of my sister is just as fierce as I recall.

"Please, help me get to Laurie and leave this place." My voice cracks. "The stars will lead us to one another. This is not the end for us."

She kisses my forehead. "I will always find you, cara mia." She pulls herself to her knees and holds me under my arms. "I am so sorry if this hurts."

It does not. There is no more pain as Marcella pulls my body across the floor and lays me next to Laurie. She places his hand in mine, and I use the last bit of my strength to squeeze it.

"I will find you, Chiara."

With my last breath, I am unafraid as I let the flames embrace me.

ACT FOUR

BROOKLYN, NEW YORK

JUNE 1887

SCENE ONE

BROOKLYN

TODAY IS THE DAY.

After ninety-one years, I will finally be reunited with Marcella.

I have been awake since yesterday, having spent the night tossing and turning; the star-shaped scar on my chest has been practically aflame with both excitement and anxiety. It pulses stronger with each passing hour, letting me know that my sister grows nearer.

The dreams began a few months ago at the vernal equinox— dreams of two young women brought together by tragedy, then ripped apart by another. They each bore the same scar that has been with me since birth, but their marks were created by sheer will.

At first, the dreams seemed to be some fantastical story, but there is nothing in my life beyond my scar to inspire such vivid dreams. Mama always told me to listen to my dreams because their messages hold power and answers to questions we have not yet asked.

So, I did. I began recording them in my journal in painstaking detail, never leaving out even the smallest details, no matter how innocuous or trivial they seemed. By the end of Spring, these visions of the past became more than mere dreams. They became memories— memories of lives gone by.

They are the memories of two women who share a soul.

I am one of those women.

My true name is Chiara Davazati. Today, my sister, by magic and by choice, Marcella Pallacioni, returns to me.

"Aye! El! Elsie!" A thick Brooklyn accent floats through my open window.

I check the time. Half past eight. Rats! I run to my bedroom window and lean out to find my friend Teddy standing three floors below on the fire escape. He is slightly obscured by various other tenants' laundry hanging over railings, blowing around like sails in the early-summer breeze.

"Gee whiz, Teddy! I'm getting ready!" I yell down.

"What is that racket?" Signora De Marco's white hair pops out of her window below. "You two, again! Always with the hollering."

I sit and straddle the window with one leg hanging out and smile sweetly at the older woman. She's full of piss and vinegar, and I love her dearly. She feels familiar to me, like I have known her in another life. Perhaps I have.

"Oh, Signora De Marco, you would miss us if we weren't here!" I tease her. "Who would bring you that cheese you love so much from the market?"

"Ah!" She suddenly disappears from view, and I pull a face at Teddy while he stands impatiently with his arms crossed. A moment later, she rejoins us, waving a small change purse. "Come take this. Bring me back tomatoes and bread." Teddy climbs the stairs to retrieve the coins, swiping the bag and giving it a shake.

"This feels heavy, Sofia." He waggles his eyebrows flirtatiously at the tiny woman, who could very well be our grandmother. "I think perhaps you could treat us to a bottle of whiskey. Ow! Ow! Stop that!"

A laugh bursts from me as Signora De Marco smacks Teddy several times. I clutch my side and almost slip right out of the window. "Whoa!" Throwing my hand up, I catch myself on the window frame above before I tumble onto the metal stairs.

"You mind yourself!" The older woman snatches the coin purse back from Teddy, giving him another smack on the back of his head for good measure. "Elsie, come down here and take this." She beckons me downstairs, waving the purse at me.

"I'll just come to your door. Let me put my shoes on." I slip back into my apartment and finish dressing, pulling on boots and piling my wild curls under a cap. I tuck my sleeveless blouse into the waistband of my trousers and grab my satchel and key.

On Tuesday mornings, Teddy and I go to the market under the East River Bridge. It's my favorite day to go since I do not work Monday evenings at the tavern. And today is extra special.

My most recent vision featured Marcella arriving on the Fulton Ferry after a long journey from Ireland. The Ferry landing is right by the market, and I plan to meet her and welcome her to New York. It's unlikely she will have a place to stay, so I will offer for her to move into the vacant apartment across the hall.

I'm positively giddy to see her, but also a tad nervous that she will not remember me— remember us.

But she will. I know it.

Bounding down the flight of stairs, my heavy footsteps echo around the narrow halls. I skid to a halt outside Signora De Marco's apartment, almost running into her as she meets me at the door. She thrusts her change purse into my hand.

"Grazie, cara mia. Get yourself a pastry. Put some meat on those bones." She grips my bicep and jiggles it, tutting at me. "No. This will not do."

I try not to roll my eyes at her and instead lean in and peck her cheek with a quick kiss. Signora De Marco is intent on feeding me until I burst every time I see her. I take my dinner with her most evenings that I do not work at Malone's Pub. "Oh, Sofia. I eat plenty enough with you around." I pocket the purse and straighten my cap. "We'll be back before supper."

Teddy is waiting for me outside. The day is already busy, the street alive with the city's song. Carriages roll along the cobblestone streets, newsboys run to and fro delivering their papers, and people call out to one another as they make their way to their destinations. The air is heavy with waste and horse manure. I would love to say that I have grown accustomed to the smell in the three years since I moved to Brooklyn, but my poor nose has not experienced such luck.

You learn to ignore it, though.

Teddy leans against a lamp post, eating a piece of toast. "About time. What were you doing in there? All of the good spots will be taken." He pushes off the post and grabs my hand, dragging me down the street.

"Teddy! You're going to tear my arm off!" I stumble, trying to keep up with him. No one will take my favorite spot, and I don't require much space.

Against my protests, Teddy drags me through the crowded streets for a few blocks until we make it to the East River Bridge. We only have one near miss with a carriage today. Teddy yelled profanities at the carriage driver that made even me blush, even though it was absolutely Teddy's fault for running into the street without waiting for an opening.

The usual fragrance of human waste begins to mingle with the strong scent of fish and yeast as we approach the market under the bridge. Merchants are set up at their stalls selling produce, fish, oils, housewares, and more. I take a few coins from Signora De Marco's purse and place them in Teddy's hand. "Get the tomatoes and bread before everything is picked over. I'll meet you at our spot."

"If it's open!" he calls over his shoulder before disappearing into the bustling crowd of merchants and patrons.

I feel at home in the chaos. My usual spot is empty, just as I suspected it would be. I tuck myself in between Teresa Lombardi and Mr. Williams. Teresa has the best cheese in New York, in my opinion, and Mr. Williams sells a wide variety of knick-knacks. I make a mental note to look through his inventory before I leave for the day— I never know what hidden treasures I will find among his piles of wares.

I straighten the crate I use as a table and dust off the two smaller milk crates that act as stools. Digging through my satchel, I find a candle, a square of an old bed sheet, and my tarot deck. Using the scrap of fabric as a tablecloth, I situate my items and pat down my pockets for my box of matches, but find my pockets empty.

"Rats!"

"Ah-hem." I look up, and a match is inches from my face. Teresa smirks down at me. "Forgot matches again, did you, Miss Elsie?"

Grateful for her kindness, I take the match. "No. I just know how much you enjoy supplying me with matches. I could never deny you the gratification."

Shaking her head, she smiles. Her dark hair is pinned up under a pale blue kerchief. Teresa isn't much older than me, perhaps twenty-five to my twenty-two years. Her family emigrated to New York years ago from Naples. She is a first-generation American and lives in Brooklyn with her husband, Francesco. They had an arranged marriage, but have managed to find happiness with each other.

Their daughter, Giovanna, is bundled to her chest. The little girl is just a few months old with a gorgeous head of black hair and a darling, round face. She coos, her big brown eyes shining, and my heart melts just a little.

I tickle her cheek with my pinkie finger, and she squirms and buries her face in her mother's breast. "Hello there, little one. Are you behaving for your momma?"

Teresa beams with pride. "She is perfect. She can sleep through the loudest noise this city can throw at her. I only wish I could do the same."

I sit on my crate and shuffle my cards. "Shall I pull a card for you, Teresa?"

She hands me a chunk of Parmigiano Reggiano wrapped in a bit of cloth as payment and I inhale its nutty fragrance, practically drooling.

I pull a card and flip it over. "The Six of Pentacles," I tell her. "I see Francesco is providing you with much love and support. This is a time of prosperity for your business. Do not forget to be generous with your success. The neighborhood is changing. It's growing, and many do not have what is necessary to find comfort as they build their new lives. These are the people who will benefit the most from your kindness."

She hands me a bundle of burrata. "Then I may as well begin with you, dear Elsie."

"That's not necessary!"

"Please. Take it. The cards do not lie."

I nod and place the cheeses in my bag. I will give the burrata to Sofia, she will be over the moon to have it.

Some of my usual customers come in a steady stream throughout the morning, paying me however they can— be it a few coins or in trade for produce or household supplies, like oil or candles. Unfortunately, the electricity in my building is unreliable at the best of times, so I still require other means for light.

Teddy comes and goes throughout the morning, earning coins as he helps elderly patrons carry their goods back to their homes in the neighborhood.

It is just past noon when I feel the pull in my chest. It's been growing steadily over the weeks as Marcella has journeyed across the sea, but this is different. The accompanying feeling is one of solace, like being wrapped in your mother's embrace by the fire on a cold evening. I smile to myself, but the moment is fleeting.

The spell my former self cast in the kitchen of our first home bound us together for eternity. Our life in Paris ended in tragedy. As did Laurence's. He has not returned to me in this life, but just like Marcella, pieces of Laurie still live within me. My dreams of him told of a beautiful life together, and I will hold him dear in this life and every life to come.

Wiping an errant tear from my eye, I send a blessing into the universe for Laurie, for Cat, and for Odette. Shuffling my cards, I close my eyes and concentrate on this new opportunity for Marcella and me to capture happiness. I sit with this thought and let it wash over me, filling me with hope.

This life will be different. I flip over the top card on my deck.

The Star.

This will be a time of healing from the wrongs and abuses of our previous lives together. This time, we may get it right and live out our wildest dreams.

I blow out my candle and hastily gather my belongings, shoving them back into my satchel with my bounty for the day: cheeses, apples, a handful of raspberries, a honeycomb, Sofia's tomatoes and bread, fresh rosemary, a candle, and a broken pocket watch from Mr. Williams that I will have repaired. Teddy is off on some errand or another, and I cannot wait for him as I spy the Fulton Ferry making its crossing across the East River from Manhattan.

It's time.

My body is buzzing with nervous energy as I weave through the market and make my way to the ferry landing at Fulton Street. A stack of crates invites me to sit and await my sister's arrival. I hop up and take an apple from my bag, dangling my legs from my perch as I chomp on my lunch and wait for the passengers to disembark.

Slowly, exhausted-looking passengers overloaded with valises and other travel bags walk toward me. Their auras vary in color and tone—some are overcome with trepidation, others with wonder and eagerness. And then I spy the one I know as surely as I know the beat of my own heart.

Her emerald-green brilliance glows brightly among the rainbow of auras. Marcella's dark brown waves are coiled atop her head, with pieces that fell free in the breeze framing her round face. She doesn't carry much on her, just a valise and travel bag with a floral pattern that she clutches close to her side.

Marcella is beautiful as ever. Her skirt is simple and grey, and her blue blouse is unbuttoned partway, no doubt to provide some relief in the midday sun.

Her brown eyes are narrowed in quiet determination as she walks toward me with her head held high. She doesn't look at me, though. She is staring past me at the landscape beyond: Brooklyn, her new home. When she is just a few yards away, I hop down from my spot and wipe apple juice from my chin. The movement catches her eye, and she stops in her tracks, appraising me.

"Well, it's about time you arrived!" I call out. Marcella looks around, confused. She doesn't know me. My heart sinks slightly. This will be a little more difficult than I had hoped, but I am nothing if not persistent. "I was thinking to myself this morning, Elsie, that apartment across the hall needs a resident with better hygiene than the last. Perhaps someone who doesn't yell profanities at the children downstairs." I take the last bite of my apple and toss the core into a nearby trash bin, then take another from my bag and hold it out to Marcella.

She approaches tentatively, rubbing at her chest with her free hand. I bite my lip, trying with all my might to suppress an excited laugh that begs for release. She has the star mark. This will work. In time, she will remember.

Our fingers touch as she takes the fruit, and it is as though a jolt of electricity is sent coursing through my veins. She quickly pulls back, almost dropping the apple. She takes a moment to compose herself.

"You say you have a place for me to live?" Her thick Irish accent rolls gracefully from her tongue, poetic in its rhythm.

The tension I didn't realize I was holding in my shoulders releases on my exhale. "I do. I'm Elsie Russo."

"Honora," she says, before shaking her head quickly. "I mean, Nora. Nora Taggart."

I smile knowingly. "They made you change your name?"

She sighs. "It's fine. Really." She doesn't sound as though it is, and if she is truly Marcella as I know her, she likely put up a fight about it.

"Honora is quite beautiful, but Nora…Nora is a name that commands attention." Her eyes perk up at that, and I extend a hand to her. "Welcome to Brooklyn, Nora Taggart. Let's go home."

She looks at my hand for a moment, pockets her apple, and we walk hand in hand on the first day of our new life.

SCENE TWO

BROOKLYN

NORA AND I WALK through the neighborhood together, and I carry her valise as I navigate our way through the crowded streets. I can tell she's overwhelmed. Brooklyn is a far cry from the provincial life she led in Ireland. She tells me about her journey and the job she will start soon as a governess to a family in Brooklyn Heights. She will earn a good wage working in that part of town. They're real uppity, lots of "nouveau riche" who have forgotten what it is like to live in the neighborhood.

We finally arrive at the apartment building, and I take her inside to talk with our landlord, Mr. McGreavy. The squat older man is in the upstairs hall sweeping the floor when we arrive. His face is hardened by time and working himself to the bone, but he is kinder than most other landlords in the neighborhood. He treats us fairly and is not prejudiced against immigrants like so many tend to be these days. "Mr. McGreavy! It is your lucky day!" I call out in a sing-song melody.

He sets his broom against the wall and crosses his arms. "Elsie, what do ya want?"

I gesture to Nora. "This is Nora Taggart. She is new to the city, and I know you wanted a much more respectable resident in the apartment across from me after the disaster with Able. There is no finer resident in all of Brooklyn than Nora."

He looks her up and down, and Nora has the good sense not to back down from his stare. She stands a little taller, taking up space and making her presence felt.

"Rent's thirty-five dollars per month. United States dollars. Don't be late."

"Mr. McGreavy! Thirty-five is outrageous, and you know it," I scold him. "I pay thirty, and that apartment needs cleaning and fixing up. There is a hole in the kitchen wall!"

"Which is why I need thirty-five. Fixes don't come cheap, missy."

I cross my arms. "Twenty-five a month."

"You tryin' to take me for broke, missy? I can raise your rent, too."

"Elsie, I can surely—" Nora starts, but I nudge her in her ribs to quiet her.

"You won't raise my rent. Who will bring you bourbon? You know I get the best bourbon at the pub. In fact, I think my rent should go down on account of the service I provide." I tap my chin thoughtfully. "Or maybe I should just go down the street and talk to Mr. and Mrs. Fratelli. They have a really nice view of Lady Liberty from their top floor."

Mr. McGreavy's bushy eyebrows raise to his dwindling hairline. His craggy face pinches as he mulls over my threat. He has a feud with the Fratellis. I do not know the entire history, but I believe they may have been business partners once upon a time.

"Twenty-nine a month. I won't go a penny lower."

I lean down and kiss my landlord's cheek. "You're a good man, McGreavy."

"I'm a soft man, is what I am." He rubs the spot where I kissed him, but he is blushing something fierce. "Head upstairs, I'll fetch the key and lease for you to sign, Miss Taggart."

Nora shakes his hand. "Thank you. I appreciate your kindness."

He waves his hand, dismissing us. "Go on."

"I need to make one stop." I lead Nora to the end of the hall and knock on the door. Sofia answers, wearing a housecoat and moccasins. I hand over her tomatoes, bread, and change purse. "Here you go! And, one more thing." I hand over a bit of cloth. She peels back the fabric, and her eyes sparkle with delight.

"Che meraviglia! Burrata!"

"It's from Teresa." Sofia disappears back into her apartment but leaves her door open. She shuffles back a moment later with a beautifully knitted yellow blanket.

"Here. Give this to Teresa. For the bambina." Her eyes flit to Nora, who is standing behind me in the hall. "Who is this?" She pushes past me into the hall, sending me crashing into the door, and takes Nora's face in her hands.

Nora looks at me with wide eyes. I give her a small shrug. It would take an act of God to stop Sofia De Marco from entering a person's personal space; I've learned to accept that she acts on impulse. She has a good soul, though. She is kind and generous, if not a little rough around the edges.

"Such a pretty face, this one has. Sofia De Marco. Supper is at six-thirty. You will join me." It was a statement, as everything is with Sofia. She is one of the only people I dare not say 'no' to.

"Nora Taggart."

"Irish. Good, good."

I step between the women. "Well, Signora, Nora has had a long journey. I'm going to get her off her feet and settled in before I must leave for work."

"Six-thirty, young lady." Her door closes with a click.

"Really, do not be late. She is a stickler for punctuality. Come on, we're one more floor up."

I unlock my apartment and usher Nora in. I set her valise by the door and take her on a brief tour of the small space. Her apartment mirror's my own. My living area has a small kitchenette with running water and a stove, a table with mismatched chairs, and a divan. A cupboard sits against one wall, donning my trinkets and a few family heirlooms.

My bedroom has just a bed with a metal frame and a small wardrobe, and I am lucky to have a small bathing chamber with running water. Much of my decor has come by way of trade at the market— a few paintings from local street artists, vases, and other items from Mr. Williams. I made the curtains myself from bed sheets and bits of lace. They do not offer much privacy from the apartments across the alley, but it is good enough.

"Your apartment looks the same as mine. You are welcome to stay here until you can buy furniture. I can take you to the market tomorrow morning if you are free. When do you begin your job?"

Nora practically falls onto the divan and leans over, placing her head to her knees. Her breath comes fast and ragged. I rush to her side and place a comforting hand on her back, rubbing in slow circles.

"Nora? What's wrong?" I ask softly, knowing full well she is on the verge of breaking down. Her energy is erratic. I can feel her heart pounding beyond the beat of my own. She is clearly overwhelmed and exhausted from her long journey and new surroundings.

She sniffles and turns her head to peer up at me, eyes glassy with tears. "I'm sorry, Miss Elsie. You must think me hysterical! Look at me crying when you have been so kind."

My heart tugs at her distress. I fish a handkerchief from my pocket and offer it to her. She takes it and dabs at her eyes. "You are *not* hysterical. You are tired and a bit overwhelmed. Nothing a meal and a good night of sleep won't fix. And please, call me El. My friends call me El." A memory of a young man named Martin crosses my mind. It warms my soul how notes of my many lives seem to repeat, reminding me that through it all, I am still Chiara Davazati at heart.

Her face brightens at the notion of us being friends, and I feel her heart slow its pace. "Thank you, El. I cannot help but think that I have made a mistake, leaving my life an ocean away to come here. The money I exchanged will not take me as far as I hoped."

"Nora, my dear, you are in luck! I know how this city works. You'll live like a queen with me around!"

Her laugh is genuine and from her belly. It's melodic and familiar.

"That sounds grand." We both look up at the quick rapping on my door. It will be Mr. McGreavy.

I give Nora's shoulders a quick squeeze and let the landlord in.

He looks stricken by Nora's tears. "Miss, are you quite alright?"

She stands, smooths her skirt, and quickly swipes at her tears. "Yes, sir. Just a bit tired."

He nods to her and hands over the key to her apartment. "Come along, then, don't have all day."

She follows him out, and I tail behind, giving some space as she enters her apartment for the first time. I peek in behind Mr. McGreavy, and I am stunned. He *is* growing soft.

The floor has been swept clean of the mouse droppings. He covered the hole in the kitchen wall with a small painting of sunflowers, and a fairly clean mattress lies propped up on pallets near the fireplace. The settee has seen better days, but it can be covered with a blanket until Nora can buy something more fitting.

None of these furnishings were here after the last tenant vacated. I thought Mr. McGreavy was going to set fire to the apartment because of how dirty it was.

"What do you think, Nora?" I ask, adding some excitement to my tone, hoping she will feel it as well.

She turns to face us, and we are met with the same determination I saw when she exited the ferry this afternoon. "It's perfect. Thank you, Mr. McGreavy."

He grunts in response, but I know it is his grunt of approval. I step back across the hall to gather Nora's belongings while she settles the lease agreement. She pays the first month of rent, and I bustle around her apartment, brightening the space with some of my own belongings: a blanket for her bed, a vase for the kitchen, and a cornicello for luck and to ward off dark energy.

She is unpacking her belongings and humming to herself. This feels...

right. Flashes of our life together in Italy are at the forefront of my mind. Fate brought us back together. Our hearts beat steady and strong, and I wonder if Nora is experiencing any memories or feelings of déjà vu. Does the peace and rhythm of us existing in the same space feel familiar?

By the time we are finished setting up her apartment, it is time for me to leave for the pub, and Nora needs to get ready for supper with Signora De Marco. "Rats! I am sorry I can't stay, but I need to get to the pub." I head over to the door, but stop in my tracks to remind her, "Don't forget, six-thirty supper. If you are late, Sofia will be personally offended. Also, do not go too early. Six-thirty exactly."

Nora surprises me by wrapping me in a hug. "Thank you, El. You are a godsend."

I hug her back, and for the first time in this lifetime, I know what it feels like to be whole. The missing piece of my heart is right here in my arms, and this time… this time we will get it right.

SCENE THREE

BROOKLYN

"WHAT'RE YA HAVIN'?" I yell over the quick tempo of the song coming from the pianist in the corner of the pub.

Fred, our usual musician, is playing some Irish jig or another, and a few boys from the neighborhood are gathered around him, hollering the words and clapping in time. They are boisterous and completely off-key.

I love it.

I have worked at Malone's for two years. It barely pays enough for me to make ends meet, but Mr. Malone does not frown upon tipping as other establishments do, and he pays extra for other odd jobs, like laundering the towels and running errands for him and his wife. With the extra from him and my days at the market, I am better off than most in the neighborhood.

I usually eat dinner with the kitchen staff, and it does not come out of my wages. Séamus's mutton stew is my favorite food in the world. Does it taste better because it is free and I did not have to prepare it myself? Perhaps.

"Gimme a lager and a whiskey." The man slides his coins across the bar to me with a wink. His fingers are stained with grease, his beard is a few days overgrown, but he has kind blue eyes. He has been here a few times and is becoming one of my regulars. "Keep the change for yourself, ma'am," he says, flashing a wide, toothy smile.

He is also a shameless flirt.

I tuck a stray lock of hair behind my ear and take his coins. "You keep trying to flatter me, and I may swoon." I return his wink, and his cheeks turn rosy.

I pour his drinks, and he leans across the bar. "I'd settle for your name, ma'am," he calls over the music.

"Her name is Elsie, and she's nothing but trouble. Will get you in the soup, this one."

Ugh. Teddy.

Putting my hands on my hips, I cock my head slightly to the side. "I must be to hang around with the likes of you, Theodore Sullivan. Now, shove off if you're not gonna order something."

He takes up the spot next to the man and orders an ale. I bring him his beer, and knowing it will wind him up, I introduce myself formally to the man. "Elsie Russo."

"Well, Miss Russo, if I am not being too forward, I'd love to call on you sometime."

Teddy chokes on his beer, and I shoot him a warning glare, then turn my attention back to my suitor. "I have so many gentlemen callers these days. It will be difficult to tell you apart from the others without your name."

"Name's Jonathan Turner. Pleased to make your acquaintance, Miss Russo."

"I can't watch this." Teddy groans and wanders off with his ale toward the group at the piano.

With my pest of a friend gone, I focus on Jonathan. He is handsome, with sandy blonde hair and a mischievous smile. He is certainly not the first man in the bar to ask to call on me, but he is most polite, and his smile makes butterflies dance in my belly. His energy is good.

"Don't mind, Teddy," I say with a wave of my hand. "He is uncouth, but basically harmless. And I would love for you to call on me. I don't have a telephone in my building, though." Telephones are a luxury I cannot hope to have for quite some time, seeing as how I am blessed by the All Mother that I even have running water.

"That's alright. May I meet you here on Sunday afternoon, say one o'clock?" He looks hopeful.

"See you then, Jonathan. Enjoy your drink." I lightly touch the back of his hand, then move to serve the patrons who have just seated themselves at the other end of the bar.

The rest of the night moves along without much fanfare. A steady stream of patrons comes and goes: factory workers unwinding after a long day, couples dining, and a few widowers who regularly meet to have a beer and play cards.

I am honestly anxious to return home to see Nora. I am doubtful that she will still be awake at this hour after such a harrowing day, but it would be good to hear about her dinner with Sofia.

I just want to know that my sister is settled in and feeling better. It is difficult for me to connect to her heart amidst the bustle and racket of the pub, but she is there. Faintly.

Teddy remains until closing time, lending a hand putting up chairs and mopping the floors. He doesn't give me any guff about Jonathan, to my great surprise. He may give me grief sometimes, but he is the closest thing I have ever had to a brother, and I know he is protective of me.

We survive the city together, helping one another with odd jobs and sharing what we earn at the market. He's family.

After the bar is clean and locked up for the night, it is after midnight. Teddy and I walk the three blocks to our apartment arm in arm in companionable silence. There is a warm breeze, and a waning moon shines brightly above. The neighborhood is peaceful at this time, its residents sleeping soundly after a hard day of work. Despite my own exhaustion, it is my favorite time of day.

It's tranquil. Families are reunited after a long day apart, safe and sound in their homes. Brooklyn is never quiet, but the noise is different: a crying baby wakes their mother to be fed, a dog barks, cats paw through garbage. The rumbling of a train cuts through the night, hushed voices carry through open windows, and water laps at the river banks.

I cannot wait to share this life with Marcella…Nora.

I cannot wait until we return to ourselves – until I can be Chiara again.

"We have a new neighbor," I say casually.

"Yeah?"

"Across the hall from me."

Teddy guffaws. "What brave soul moved into *that* disaster?"

"Irish immigrant. Nora Taggart. If you can believe it, Mr. McGreavy fixed up the place for her. Best he could, anyway. Even gave her a mattress and some other furniture from storage."

My friend gapes at me, shocked to his core at our landlord's uncharacteristic behavior. "He must be quite taken with her. That old grump doesn't do anyone that type of kindness without conditions. It must be a cold day in the depths of Hell."

"I *may* have threatened to send Nora to speak with the Fratellis if he didn't treat her fairly."

"And?"

"And I kissed his cheek. He turned red as an apple."

He gasps in mock surprise. "The scandal! Miss Russo, using your feminine wiles to get your way. Do people ever actually tell you 'no'?"

I shrug. "Hardly ever."

Teddy playfully shoves me, sending me stumbling toward the street, but catches me before I meet the dirt-covered cobblestones of Fulton Street. "Sorry, El. Didn't mean to give you such a hard push there."

Grasping at his arm to haul myself to stand straight, I huff at him in exasperation, muttering under my breath. "And you think *I'm* a nuisance."

When we finally arrive home, the building is quiet as a church mouse. I leave Teddy at his door and walk the additional two flights upstairs, pausing at Nora's door to listen for movement, but all is still. Disappointed, I turn to unlock my own door and hear the creak of wood behind me.

"Elsie?" a voice asks softly.

My heart lightens at her voice. I school my face, not wanting to appear too eager to see Nora and turn to greet her. "Nora. I'm surprised to see you are still awake. Is everything alright?"

She sighs. "No. I mean, yes. I mean…" her shoulders sink with another sigh. She is wearing a white dressing gown and her hair is plaited over her shoulder. "Would you think me childish if I said that I am afraid? Well, maybe not afraid, but *uneasy*. It's a new place, and I feel out of sorts and alone."

I offer her a small smile and shake my head. "I felt the same when I moved." I open my door and look over my shoulder. "You coming?"

Nora's smile could light up the whole of Brooklyn. She locks her door and hurries in behind me. She falls asleep almost as soon as she lies on the divan. I cover her with a blanket and go to my own bed. Sleep takes me quickly. I dream of painting in the French countryside, Marcella at my side, covered in ink as she pens a novel under the name of another.

SCENE FOUR

BROOKLYN

IT HAS BEEN ONE week since Marcella arrived in New York. For the first few days, I introduced her to our neighbors and helped her furnish the apartment, with Teddy begrudgingly helping haul furniture and other goods up the three flights of stairs. I then escorted her to meet the family she is working for and helped her find the most efficient route to work.

The family is quite posh. Nora will spend three nights per week in their home to tutor their children, and will spend two additional days caring for them and taking them on outings. She is not required to stay those nights in their home and has most weekends to herself, though she will need to work some weekends and nights when her employers have events to attend in the city.

She began her job yesterday, and I unfortunately will not see her again until Thursday evening when she arrives home.

I have not approached the topic of Marcella and Chiara with her. The move has been a lot to bear, and she needs time to find her footing in her new life.

I suspect she must feel *something,* though.

We have spent every night since that first night sleeping in the same apartment, either mine or her own. Our time together is comfortable. We laugh and talk about our lives before we came to Brooklyn, and make plans for all of the exciting things we will experience together in New York: getting dressed up and going to shows, picnics in Central Park, and days by the shore.

I ate dinner with Nora and Sofia the nights I did not work at the pub. Teddy was kind enough to have supper with Nora the other evenings, though I do not think it was an imposition. He is clearly sweet on her and blushes when she smiles at him.

I spent Sunday afternoon with Jonathan, and it was quite lovely. He is a gentleman, and conversation comes easily between us. We walked across the East Street Bridge promenade and had lunch at a café in the city. We agreed to see each other again this coming Sunday, but I suspect that I will see him at Malone's before then.

This evening at work rolls by slower than molasses. The pub is unusually quiet, just a few of our regular patrons scattered about. Fred tinkles at the piano keys halfheartedly, lacking his usual vigor when he has an audience of loaded young men fresh from a day at the factory or docks.

I have been absently wiping down the same section of the bar for the last five minutes. The kitchen door swings open, prompting me to straighten my posture and scrub with a little more *oompf*.

"Ah, Miss Elsie, I know yer slacking about. It's dead as a doornail in here. Why don't ya take off? I'll take over minding the bar."

"Are you sure? I can help clean in the kitchen," I offer.

Mr. Malone makes a motion with his hand, silently telling me to skedaddle. "Thank you, sir. I will see you Thursday morning for laundry?"

He nods and hums in agreement. "Goodnight, Miss Elsie. Do you want me to send Fred to walk you home?" He glances at our pianist, who is currently sitting with his face propped up in one hand while playing a morose tune with the other hand.

"I would never deny you the pleasure of his musical splendor." I bite down a laugh at Mr. Malone's scowl.

"I can hear you, Miss Elsie." Fred stands, closes the piano, and quickly downs his beer in one gulp. "I'll see you to your apartment, safe and sound."

Fred walks me home and leaves me at my door with a curt nod, and I race up the stairs to my apartment. After cleaning myself up, I sit near the open window with my journal and an oil lamp, and begin to write, grateful for the cool evening breeze.

June 14, 1887

Marcella arrived just a week ago. She has not yet regained her memories, and I have not pressed her to do so. I know in the deepest depths of my soul that she feels the tether that binds us. While we are still strangers in this life, there is an undeniable connection. We have spent every free moment together, and it feels as though hardly any time has passed. She is still Marcella, if not a little reserved as Nora, but I see her strength. Forever the caregiver and woman who longs for a life beyond her time. In every life, Marcella strives for something beyond the confines society has thrust upon us, and this life is no exception.

Perhaps we will finally break free of the chains of man and live for ourselves.

Perhaps this life will be the life we dared to dream of when we were but children who knew nothing of the world except that it held possibility.

I set down my pen and place a mug on my journal to hold it open while the ink dries. A thought prickles at me. What is it that I actually desire? I have a vague notion of what a life should be, but it is difficult to reconcile with the lives I have lived.

An apothecary, an artist hiding in plain sight, a revolutionary.

A wife.

A sister.

I am not so different from Marcella. I want more. I have *been* more. I need more.

I am just uncertain what "more" consists of in the present. All of my dreams are of the past.

It is time to dream of a future.

SCENE FIVE

BROOKLYN

"I AM THOROUGHLY EXHAUSTED. I believed traveling across the Atlantic would be the most difficult ordeal of my life. I was naive." Nora lies haphazardly across her settee with her feet in my lap. My friend's dress is in complete disarray and rumpled around her thighs, and her hair is a fright, falling out of its normally severe bun in loose waves around her face. The skirt of her floral-patterned dress is stained with a variety of substances I dare not attempt to identify.

Rubbing her feet, I contemplate asking what demons possess the children in her charge, but settle for a more cordial version of my question. "Are you caring for children or a litter of wolf pups?" Or not.

Nora props herself up on her elbows and pins me with a look that is somehow simultaneously a scowl and a look of utter helplessness. "Never in all my life have I encountered such wild beings. To come from such wealth and act like rabid dogs is beyond my comprehension. It is clear to me now why they searched for a governess from across the sea. All of New York must already be aware that their children are beasts."

I throw my head back, unable to control my laughter. I underestimated my sister. Fire still burns hotter than the sun within her. "If it helps at all, I had no idea the beast children existed. I don't run in circles that would expose me to that family. They're not exactly patrons at Malone's."

"Speaking of, I do not have work this weekend. Would you mind terribly if I visited you at the pub? It may bring me some comfort and a sense of home."

"Not at all! It's not exactly Delmonico's, but our cook is fabulous. His mutton stew is my favorite food in all of Brooklyn."

Nora leans back again, eyes closed, humming in appreciation. "I do miss my mother's stew."

"Then it's settled. You will join me tomorrow evening. You can walk with Teddy. I'll let him know when we go to the market in the morning." I hide my excitement to have Nora at the pub. I'm a little more than eager to see how she conducts herself in such a casual setting.

I glance at the clock that sits on her mantle. It's growing late, and I have a long day ahead of me tomorrow. "I should go. Between the market and Malone's, tomorrow shall be an exceedingly long day." Nora looks as disappointed as I feel. She swings her legs around to the floor so that I can stand.

She joins me and takes both of my hands.

"I cannot thank you enough, El, for all that you have done for me. You have made a frightening and overwhelming experience easier. I just want you to know how much I appreciate you, and that I will never forget the kindness you have shown me. You are a true friend, perhaps the truest I have ever known."

A shimmering, golden light pulses around us, and my heart beats steady and strong in time with hers. I pull Nora to me and hug her as a tear slides down my cheek. "And you are my truest friend, my dear Nora." We straighten ourselves, and she escorts me to the door. I hesitate, not wanting to spend another night apart when I just got her back. "I will see you tomorrow night. Sleep well, Nora."

"Goodnight, El."

SCENE SIX

BROOKLYN

MALONE'S IS FILLED TO the brim tonight, so much so that I am growing hoarse from yelling over the raucous crowd and Fred's jovial pounding of the keys. I spy Nora and Teddy laughing and dancing in the open space by the piano. He is swinging her around, and I long to join them.

"Do you have a moment to spare a dance?" My belly warms, and I turn to face Jonathan, who has managed to slide into a small space between two men seated at the bar.

He cleans up good. His hair is neatly combed, and his beard is trimmed close to his face. Before I answer, I pour him a whiskey and slide it across the bar.

"If only." I gesture to the sea of bodies that require my attention. "I can't recall the last time it was this busy." I dab my chest above my bodice with a rag. It is hotter than Hell with so many bodies crammed together in the early summer heat. I am sweating like a pig at a butcher shop, and I want nothing more than to plunge myself into a cold bath at the end of the night.

Jonathan's face falls a little. He cups his hands around his mouth. "Malone!" My boss looks over from his spot at the other end of the bar. Jonathan waves him over.

"Yeah?"

"Could I please borrow Miss Russo for just a few minutes to join me in a dance?"

Mr. Malone looks to me for confirmation that I would indeed like to dance with Jonathan. Seeing my pleading eyes, the corner of his mouth ticks up just a hair, and he nods. "Go on. One dance, Miss Elsie."

I jump up in triumph and race around the bar. "Thank you!" I call back to Mr. Malone and meet Jonathan, dragging him to the dance floor, where we join Teddy and Nora. Jonathan spins me and leads me in quick steps to the tempo. The patrons around us clap and stomp their feet, whistling and hollering. I spy Nora out of the corner of my eye, and my jaw drops as I watch her feet moving quickly as she spins and stomps to the beat. Her hair has come free, and she is radiant as she and Teddy dance in time.

Jonathan speaks into my ear. "Come on, Elsie. Let's show them how it's done!" I am speechless as Jonathan mimics Teddy's moves. I cannot stop laughing as I join him. He grabs my hands and swings me around, and I screech with delight as I feel free and weightless, spinning in circles.

We switch partners— Jonathan dances with Nora, and I with Teddy. We switch back, over and over, swinging one another in circles. Fred ends the song with a flourish, and I practically collapse in Jonathan's arms, chest heaving and out of breath. He surprises me and kisses my cheek. His lips are soft and warm, contrasting with the roughness of his beard.

"Thank you for the dance," he murmurs. "Let's return you to Malone."

I bite my lip, and my cheeks heat in a way that has nothing to do with the stuffiness of the crowded bar, but I let him hold my hand and lead me back to my place behind the bar. He winks and walks off to talk with Teddy. I notice that he stands a little taller as he weaves through the crowd.

Breathless and hotter than ever, I down a glass of water and return to my post, filling beer steins and whiskey glasses. "El!" Nora's voice rises above the din. She is flushed and burning brightly in a gold halo of light. Her hair is wild, damp waves forming in the summer humidity. I pour her a glass of water, which she quickly gulps. "Can I get a lager?"

I choke on a laugh. Nora is full of surprises this evening. "Coming right up." I fill a mug for her.

"That was a good craic! Didye know Teddy could dance like that?"

"Honestly, no. I think you inspire him."

I glance across the way. Jonathan is speaking animatedly, but Teddy's eyes are solidly on Nora. As if she can feel his eyes on her, she peeks back over her shoulder, and Teddy quickly averts his attention back to Jonathan. I chuckle and shake my head.

"He's a sweet lad. Do ye think he fancies me?" She sips her drink and tries, but fails, to appear nonchalant. The change in Nora after a few drinks is astonishing as her proper demeanor slips away bit by bit.

I wipe up a bit of spilled beer and refill the mug of the man next to Nora. "He absolutely does."

She leans her elbows on the bar. "He is sort of handsome, do ye think?"

I lay a hand on her arm and smile gently. "If you think he is, that's what counts, right?"

She chugs down the rest of her drink and slams the mug down. "Yer right!" She looks gleeful, and I am stunned as she pushes her way through the crowd and reclaims her dance partner from Jonathan. Teddy looks almost relieved as Nora tugs on his hand and commands Fred to play something that must be a favorite.

Eventually, the crowd trickles out. I am mopping the floors, and Nora is sitting atop a table, deep in conversation with Teddy. Jonathan is still here and insists on helping, setting chairs on top of tables so that I can mop without the obstructions.

"I'm gonna get Nora home!" Teddy calls out.

"Thanks, Teddy. I'll see you both in the morning!"

Nora rushes me and hugs me tightly. "Thanks, El!" She kisses my cheek and skips off after Teddy. He guides her by the small of her back out into the night, and the door closes with a click behind them.

"She's quite something, huh?" Jonathan chuckles.

"She really is." My chest clenches for a moment, then the tightness dissipates as Nora walks further from the pub. "You don't have to help.

I'm almost done here."

"What kind of gentleman would I be if I didn't walk you home?"

I give him a half-smile. "I suppose not much of a gentleman at all." I finish up and return my mop and bucket to the kitchen, saying goodnight to the cook and Mr. and Mrs. Malone. They send me home with a package of leftover biscuits.

When I come out of the kitchen with my satchel over my shoulder, Jonathan is waiting at the door, eyes shining in the dim light of the bar. "Shall we?" he asks, holding open the door.

I skip over and link my arm through his and set off into the night.

I waste no time before eating my biscuits. I am absolutely famished, as I only had time to take a few meager bites of food throughout the night. I shove half a biscuit into my gob and hold it with my teeth while I fish out another from the paper sack and hand it to Jonathan. I cannot be bothered with manners as I devour the biscuit. Crumbs fall down my bodice, and it takes all of my self-control not to pick them out. Jonathan huffs a laugh under his breath and shakes his head.

"Do you want the rest of mine?"

I eye his half-eaten biscuit longingly and worry at my lip, wanting to say yes, but also feeling slightly awkward about taking the biscuit back after I had just given it to him.

"Elsie, go on. I can tell you want it." His lips turn up at one corner, and my heart stutters in my chest. How is everything this man does so charming?

"Thank you." I take the biscuit, but take smaller bites this time. We walk another block, not saying much while I nibble at my food. The new electric street lights cast a ghastly blue haze over the neighborhood. It is still lively, despite the late hour. Other people walk home after a night of revelry, laughing and joking about. The delicate plucking of fiddle strings floats through the air from a nearby home. Hooves clomp against the cobblestones, carrying people home from their evening out.

We reach my building, and ever the gentleman, Jonathan escorts me up the few steps to the door. I suddenly feel flustered, staring into the blue of his eyes that pierce me with yearning. The tension between us has been silently building since he kissed me back at the pub.

My breath catches as his hand cups my chin and brushes a calloused thumb across my lips. "Crumbs."

A nervous chuckle works its way from my throat. I am unsure of what I am doing. I lean back against the door, and Jonathan cages me, leaning an arm against the door frame.

"I enjoy spending time with you, El. I am utterly captivated by your beauty and charm." His thumb pulls lightly at my bottom lip, and I am transfixed like a moth to flame.

Will he kiss me? *Really* kiss me? Do I want him to? My body feels alive with electricity and the same yearning I see in his expression.

Yes. I do. My eyes flutter closed, and I stand on my tiptoes, eager to meet his mouth. Then, without warning, I am falling backwards. "Oh!" I cry out as my body slams into another.

"Miss Russo!" Mr. McGreavy catches me and hauls me upright. My entire body feels aflame with embarrassment. "Who are you?" He pushes past me and stands before Jonathan, creating a ridiculous scene as he thrusts a finger upward into Jonathan's face.

Stunned, Jonathan composes himself quickly and attempts to take Mr. McGreavy's hand to shake it. "I'm Jonathan Turn—"

"Is this man bothering you, Miss Russo?" My landlord cuts him off and turns back to me, jerking a thumb over his shoulder.

I cover my mouth with a hand to stifle a laugh and fix my face into an expression that I hope is more serious. "Jonathan was just kindly seeing me home safely from work, Mr. McGreavy."

The squat man eyes Jonathan suspiciously. "You just say the word, and I will boot him out of here."

Jonathan and I share a look over Mr. McGreavy's head of amusement.

"That won't be necessary." I move between them, saving my companion and myself from further embarrassment.

"If you say so. Well, you'd better get in here, Miss Russo. That Irish lass of yours and Teddy came in a few minutes ago, causing a commotion. I won't have you lot disturbing the building at all hours."

I wince. I clearly underestimated Nora's condition after so much giggle juice. She's more pissed than I believed. "I'll be right up to look after her."

"I have my eyes on you." Mr. McGreavy motions from his eyes to Jonathan and heads back inside.

Reluctantly, I say my goodbye. "I should go see to Nora. Thank you for the dance and for walking me home."

Jonathan raises my hand to his lips, placing a kiss on my knuckles. "Goodnight, El. I will see you on Sunday?"

"Yes. Sunday." I turn to go inside and make a rash decision. *Be bold, El.*

Without letting myself overthink it, I throw myself at Jonathan, catching him off guard, and drag his mouth down to my own. He tastes sweet and slightly spicy, with a hint of whiskey. He catches me and kisses me back gently, slowly, as though he is savoring the taste of me.

I pull back and brush a lock of his hair from his brow. "Sweet dreams, Jonathan." Before he can respond, I race inside, but I hear a whoop of enthusiasm on the other side of the door.

I take the stairs two at a time up to my floor. I raise my hand to knock on Nora's door, but she flings it open before my knuckle touches the wood. "El! Come in!"

"Ooof!" Nora drags me in from the hall and spins me around in circles.

"El! Wha' took ye so long? Teddy and I have been waiting forever for you."

A night of drink has peeled away Nora's carefully practiced enunciation like turpentine stripping paint from a wall, revealing her true accent. It's startling but also a breath of fresh air to hear Nora as she was meant to be heard.

I peer around her. "Teddy is here?"

On cue, Teddy appears from the bathing room, holding a robe. I finally take notice of the state of Nora's dress. She is wearing nothing more than her undergarments and a slip. I spin Nora and help Teddy cover her, wanting to preserve her modesty. She does not stop chattering through it all.

"Did ye know Fred knew so many of my favorite songs? He played them all!"

I tie the belt of her robe and pull it closed, covering Nora as best I can. "That's wonderful. Fred is an exceptional pianist."

"And Teddy! Teddy is the best dance partner I've eva 'ad. Teddy! Show El tha' move where ye spin me 'round."

Teddy drags a hand over his face. "Nora, I think we are done with dancing tonight. It is time for all of us to go to bed."

Nora's face falls. "Ye don't wanna dance with me?"

"Of course I do. And we will dance again next week at the pub. But right now, it is time for us to rest our dancing feet." Teddy takes Nora by the hand and leads her to her bedroom, ignoring her petulant protests. I follow behind and watch him tuck her in.

I stand behind Teddy and squeeze his shoulder. "Go on, get out of here. I will take it from here."

Teddy kisses my cheek and departs, closing Nora's bedroom door softly behind him.

"Where's Teddy goin'?" she pouts.

"Teddy is going downstairs to rest his dancing feet, and we are going to rest ours."

Nora shifts over and pats the spot next to her. "Stay with me."

She looks so childlike, curled up in the blankets. I cannot say no. Kicking off my shoes, I remove my dress and let it fall into a heap on the floor, and climb in next to Nora. She snuggles up to me. "Yer my best friend, El," she whispers and buries her head in my shoulder. She is asleep in an instant.

I kiss her forehead and lay my cheek against the top of her head. "And you are mine." The rhythmic beat of our hearts in time with each other lulls me to sleep.

SCENE SEVEN

BROOKLYN

"ELSIE?" NORA'S VOICE CROAKS. She shuffles into her kitchen and sits at the small table. She looks a fright. Her brown hair is knotted, and the skin under her eyes is shaded like a plum. I'm standing at her stove making eggs and sausages. "Everythin' is so bright and loud. Can ye make tha sun go back to bed?"

"Unfortunately, I do not have that command over the universe, despite my best efforts. Breakfast will be ready in just a moment." I turn over the sausages and remove the kettle from the flame to pour her a cup of tea.

I set the cup in front of her, and she sniffs at it, face pinched. "Wha' is it?"

"A special blend of my own. It will help with the nausea and your head."

Hesitantly, she sips and scowls. "Well, it tastes like shite."

The valerian root in the tea is strong and unpleasant against the bite of ginger, but it will help her. I spoon a bit of honey into the cup and give it a quick stir. "You will thank me when your head stops pounding." I plate our food, adding slices of bread to our plates. "Here. You need to eat."

Nora groans into her hands. "I dunno know if I can. I'm afraid it will come right back up." But she hesitantly mops up egg yolk with her bread and nibbles at it anyway. "I'm sorry, El. My behavior last night was—"

I raise a hand to stop her. "You have nothing to apologize for. We had a grand time, and I hope we do it again."

Nora takes a deep breath and sinks back into her chair. "Thank you. I hope we do as well." She pushes her food around her plate with her fork. "D'ye think Teddy is sore about last night?"

I sip my own tea, hiding my smile. "Not at all. I have taken care of a pissed Teddy on more than one occasion."

The tension in my heart loosens a bit as Nora relaxes. She eats her breakfast at a leisurely pace, but eventually cleans her plate. I draw her a bath and return to my own apartment to bathe and get dressed for the day. I have a few errands to run for Mr. Malone before my shift this afternoon, and I cannot pass on the extra pay. After a late night, I am grateful to only work for the afternoon and early evening today.

I do not see Nora much the remainder of the weekend, just in passing as we go about our respective duties. I spend Sunday with Jonathan walking in Central Park and having dinner in the city. Nora then returned to the manor to care for the children for a few days.

My date with Jonathan was wonderful. I feel so at ease with him. He is everything a woman could dream of in a husband. He is handsome, makes me laugh, and he treats me with respect and looks at me like there is no other woman in all of New York.

But something inside me knows this is not meant to be. There is an emptiness to be filled, and it cannot be filled by a life tied down to one place with one person.

This feeling nags at me throughout the week, and I withdraw into myself, trying to determine what will satiate the burning hunger that I cannot quite identify.

On Wednesday, I sit on the floor of my living area with my tarot cards. I burn dried daffodils and dandelions in a bowl to help promote clarity. Lit candles burn all around me, illuminating the space with their dancing flames.

I focus all of my energy on the deck, holding it between my hands with intention. What will the future bring me? What is it I am to do? What will bring my soul peace? Exhaling, I deal three cards.

I flip the first. The Fool. I flip the next. The Hierophant. Finally, the Six of Swords. I sit back, resting on my palms and consider the cards before me.

The Fool is a sign of new beginnings. Marcella just came back to me, and I cannot allow this opportunity of starting anew to pass me by. The All Mother blessed us with the gift to rewrite our history. Each of our lives has not been easy, but the one constant is that we have each other. We have our bond and our love. We must make that count.

The Hierophant speaks to me of the contradiction and war within my heart of reconciling what the world expects of me against what I dream of for myself. What are *my* needs? Do I sit idly by on tradition, acting the role that men have preconceived for me?

Or…

Do I win at the men's game? Georgette was bold. She did not care for the conventions of men.

And neither do I.

The Six of Swords. A time of transition and upheaval from the life I know now. I move the Six of Swords next to the Fool and tap a fingernail thoughtfully on the Fool.

The fog and uncertainty clouding my thoughts dissipate, allowing the future to become crystal clear.

I know what I must do.

As I crawl into bed with a smile upon my lips, I envision a life without boundaries where Marcella and I set out on adventures and experience all that the world has to offer.

SCENE EIGHT

BROOKLYN

"FIVE DOLLARS."

"Armand! Do I look like Queen Victoria?" I gesture at my trousers and yellow floral blouse that bears a tomato stain from my most recent supper with Sofia.

"Miss Elsie, I have a business to run. Five dollars to fix the watch." The shop owner pushes his spectacles up his narrow nose and crosses his arms.

"What if you don't fix the crack in the glass?" I point to the spider-webbed watch face.

"Then you will be right back here in a few weeks, needing the glass replaced when it shatters. Five dollars, Elsie. That's the rate."

I huff and blow a strand of hair from my eyes. I know I am acting like a child, but I cannot afford five dollars to fix the watch from Mr. Williams. "What if I bring you a bottle of bourbon from the pub in trade?"

"Five dollars, or you can leave my store."

Rats! "But Armaaaand," I drone, hoping to wear him down. "You know I cannot afford that." I rummage around in my satchel, hoping to find something worth his while for trade. "Here! Fresh mozzarella from Teresa Lombardi and two plums," I say triumphantly.

Armand looks down at me over his spectacles like I am a fly in his soup, and the hope drains from me. I set two crumpled dollar bills and two quarters on the counter next to the cheese and give him what *I think* is my most dazzling smile. Or, at least, I hope it is. It's also possible that I look like a raving lunatic, but desperate times call for desperate measures.

His shoulders droop with a heavy sigh, and I know I have him. "Bring the bourbon tomorrow. The watch will be ready."

I squeal and clap my hands. "Thank you, Armand! I always knew you were a fair and honorable man."

"Get out of my store, Elsie. I'll see you tomorrow."

I hurry to the door and spare a glance back. He is smiling and shaking his head. "Have a nice day, Armand!"

With the matter of the broken watch settled, I head to my next destination: a dress shop. I do not know what I can hope to afford, but the weather is growing hotter with each day. I need something to wear to work that will be cool. After a few minutes of perusing, I find a lavender cotton dress with lace cap sleeves that is light and airy. The silver buttons down the bodice gleam brightly at me. I know better than to haggle with the shop owner and cringe knowing how many extra jobs I will need to take on to make up for the cost.

I vow to make my next dress, though I am a terrible seamstress.

I must admit, the dress makes me feel like royalty. Purple is a color that holds power. Or perhaps I feel like royalty because I spent almost all of my savings on it.

I make two additional stops on errands for Mr. Malone, then rush home to change and go to work. I find a bit of lace in a hat box and use it to tie up my hair. Satisfied with my appearance, I shove my apron in my satchel and set off.

A low whistle catches my attention when I reach the front door. "El, is that you?"

I cannot help myself. I spin slowly, showing off my dress. "Do ya like it?"

Teddy takes my hand and spins me again. "Elsie, you almost look like a real woman."

I stomp on his foot. "Ouch! There she is."

"You would be so lucky to find a woman like me, Theodore."

"Ouch, again. Using my full name. Really, though. You look beautiful, El. Headed to work?"

"Yes."

"I'll walk with you." He takes me by the elbow and leads me out to the busy street.

I give him a dubious look. "You are acting odd."

"What do you mean? I'm just walking my dear friend to work. These streets are dangerous, you know."

I halt my steps. "You just want to be seen with me to impress people."

"Shhh! Keep your voice down and just let me be a gentleman for once in my life. I need practice."

I allow Teddy to link arms with me again. "What do you mean you need practice? *Oh.*" It dawns on me then: Teddy wants to impress Nora. "I see. Well then, let's go. Remember to open the door to the pub for me. And switch sides. You do not let a lady walk close to the street. If a runaway carriage comes along, the horse can hit you."

"On second thought, maybe I don't need the practice," he grumbles, but switches sides with me anyway.

I am extra careful all night to not spoil my dress and choose to wear an apron. I eat much more daintily than I ever have in my life when I join the kitchen staff for my dinner. Mr. Malone must have taken note of my dress because he offered me extra jobs cleaning the pub and running his errands, and two additional shifts before I even had to ask, which I gratefully accepted. It will be a busy week, but I desperately need to make up the loss.

On my walk home with Fred, I hurry him along. Nora should be home. I doubt she is awake, but I hope to see her in the morning for breakfast before she must head back to the manor.

Her apartment is dark and quiet. Disappointed, but unsurprised, I go into my own apartment. It is enough that I can feel her presence, and I sleep soundly knowing she is only across the hall.

SCENE NINE

BROOKLYN

MY HANDS ARE RED and raw from scrubbing every surface of the pub. The previous night's crowd had been especially rambunctious and left a terrible mess and broken glass when a brawl broke out. It got hairy for a minute until Mr. Malone could kick out the offenders, and the police eventually arrived.

I am actually a *little* disappointed I did not witness the entire ordeal, as my boss had shoved me back into the kitchen and demanded I stay put for my safety.

While I appreciate Mr. Malone for taking good care of me, my poor hands look like I dipped them in a vat of hot oil. I will need to do some extra haggling at the market to obtain ingredients to whip up a balm to soothe my inflamed skin.

"Miss Elsie, you're still here?" Séamus comes out of the kitchen and finds me on my hands and knees with a bucket and brush, vigorously scouring a stain on the wood floor.

I push upright and wipe the sweat from my brow with the back of my hand. "Those animals did a real number on the bar last night." I nod at the overflowing garbage bin and sink back down onto my heels. "What time is it?"

"Half past three."

Slamming down my scrub brush, I blow out an exasperated sigh. "Rats!" I was supposed to meet Nora over an hour ago. She offered to help mend a few of my dresses that are a little worse for wear.

"Go on, get out of here. I will finish up."

"Séamus, that's not fair. Mr. Malone is paying me extra to clean up."

"I'll deal with Malone. Off ye go. Here, take these." He hands me a paper sack. The heavenly scent of butter and yeast permeates through the bag. I hug Séamus and thank him before scurrying out, not caring that I look a fright, sweating and covered in filth.

I barely have my key in the door when Nora flings her own door open and accosts me in the hall. "El! Where've ye been? Are you alright?" Her eyes are wide and panicked.

"I'm fine. The bar was just such a mess, and I lost track of time. I'm sorry. I didn't mean to worry you."

Exhaling a sigh of relief, she ushers me into my own apartment, prodding me along like one of her charges. "Let's get you cleaned up, and we can begin. I'll fix you something to eat while you wash."

My scar pulses with happiness as my friend— my sister — effortlessly slips into her role as caretaker, fussing about my kitchen. I slip into my bathing room and set to washing the grime from this day off my body. I wrangle my wild curls into a plait, which I pin up off my neck. Desperate to combat the heat, I bathe with cold water.

Not caring for modesty in front of Nora, I wear nothing more than my undergarments and a slip, but ensure it is high enough to hide my scar. It is entirely too hot in my apartment, and there is not a breeze to be found coming in through the open windows.

Nora is seated at my kitchen table, dabbing at her neck with a handkerchief. A plate with sliced tomato, cheese, and bread sits across from her with a cup of water, which I greedily drink down in one go. "Thank you, Nora. Truly, I am sorry for my tardiness."

She stands to refill my cup and pours a glass of water for herself as well. "I am just glad to see you are unharmed."

"What did you think happened?" I ask around a mouthful of bread.

"I do not know. What if you had been hit by a carriage or kidnapped?"

I choke on my bread and pound on my chest with a fist a few times. "Kidnapped!" I squeak after the bread dislodges from my throat. "Nora, what tales have you heard about New York?"

"Well, there are gangs and the mob, and I know sometimes they patronize the pub. It sounds like after the night ye had, I was right to worry." She crosses her arms and raises her chin, indicating she will not accept an argument from me.

I raise my hands in surrender. "Perhaps you are just a little right," I tease, but she doesn't look amused, and I am not surprised. Marcella always played the role of the big sister after we lost our families, and she is once again slipping seamlessly into the role. I hold her hand and give it an affectionate squeeze. "Mr. Malone would never allow something to happen to me. I promise, I was never in any danger last night, but I appreciate that you care enough to worry about me. I will send a message along next time I expect to be late."

Satisfied with my answer, Nora nods curtly. "Now then, where are the dresses you need mended?"

I wince. "Well…it is all of them."

Nora crosses her legs at her ankles and sits back in her chair, sipping her water. "I am not surprised. Ye run about town like a feral child."

I nearly choke on my food again, but I see the mischief dancing in Nora's eyes over the brim of her cup and instead throw a piece of bread, hitting her square in the forehead. "I am not *feral*! I am full of life and spirit."

"Yer spirited enough to scare off a banshee." Her demeanor is calm and collected as she needles me. It feels reminiscent of another time, when Marcella would relentlessly tease me to get a rise out of me.

"You are being quite obnoxious today," I pout, shoveling another mouthful of tomato and cheese into my gob.

"Eat. I'll grab my sewing supplies."

While Nora is seated on my divan, working at patching the tears and holes in my dresses, I am sprawled on my floor with my tarot cards.

"What are you doing?" she inquires.

"Reading my cards."

Nora sets aside the blue dress she is mending, peering over me at the cards set out on the floor. "How does it work?"

I motion for her to join me on the floor. She sits carefully, tucking her legs under her and arranging her skirt so that it is not bunched. I collect the cards into a pile and hand them to her.

"Give them a shuffle," I instruct her. Awkwardly, Nora mixes up the large cards. "Now, hold them and think about something you want for yourself, or something you wish to have insight about."

She looks at me skeptically, but I give her an encouraging smile. Nora takes a deep breath and closes her eyes, holding the cards between her hands. After a moment, her eyes flutter open, and she hands me the deck.

I deal out three cards. Flipping over the first, I am stunned by the card.

"The Knight of Wands," I tell her. "This is an interesting card for you, given that you have already set out on a new adventure simply by moving to a new country. But to me, it is telling us that more adventure awaits and that you must approach it with determination and without apprehension."

"What other adventure do ye possibly think could be ahead?" Her brows knit together in thought.

I shrug noncommittally. "That is part of the adventure. It is up to you to determine what journeys are worth embarking upon. It will come to you." I turn over the next card. "Page of Pentacles." I move the card to overlap with the Knight. "What I see when we put these two cards together is that your adventure will be based on what you desire and what you strive for. What is it that will bring you contentment in your life?"

Nora worries at her bottom lip, and I can practically see her mind at work, dissecting the cards' meanings against her own ambitions.

"Shall I continue?"

Nora nods just once.

I slowly flip over the final card, and my breath hitches. "The Star," Nora and I say in unison. Her hand absently travels to the middle of her chest and comes to rest over the same spot where my scar lives.

"Ah-hem." I clear my throat and pull my attention back to the card. "The Star is symbolic of a time of rejuvenation. Perhaps the adventure on the horizon will rekindle a passion that has been lost to you over the years." I pause and choose my next words carefully. "It may be a time of rebirth for you."

Our eyes meet over the cards, a golden haze enveloping us in its embrace. I watch as Nora's expression cycles through several emotions: pensive, mystified, then finally tranquil.

"Well, that is certainly something for me to consider. What about you? What adventure is in your future, El?"

A smile creeps across my lips. "Whatever adventure may come, I just hope that we sail that sea together."

"Oh, El. I do not wish to be aboard a ship for quite some time to come." Nora looks peaked at the prospect of being trapped on a ship.

I shove her lightly. "Get your sea legs, Nora! We are bound for exotic destinations!"

We collapse on the floor in a gale of giggles, the cards and my dresses long forgotten. We lie staring at the ceiling, fingers laced together, talking about all of the wonderful and exciting places we could sail to, until my apartment is blanketed in the pale blue of the moon's splendor.

SCENE TEN

BROOKLYN

THE COOL, OCEAN BREEZE whips my hair around as I stand at the edge of the shore, letting the incoming waves jostle me about. I sink further into the sand, enjoying the feel between my toes, not caring that my skirt is soaked through.

The next wave almost sweeps my feet from under me, but Jonathan's strong arms catch me before the surf carries me away. Coney Island is bustling with families and children shrieking with joy and splashing in the water. Gulls fly overhead, squawking and causing mayhem with their fearless determination to disrupt picnickers.

Another wave comes in and knocks us both on our behinds. I screech as the ocean swallows me, grabbing onto Jonathan for purchase. The water recedes, and he drags me to my feet. We are both roaring with laughter so hard we can barely stand upright.

I collapse onto the sand a few yards from the incoming tide, and Jonathan plops down beside me. "Well. We are properly soaked." My cheeks ache from smiling and laughing. My hair is dripping wet and full of sand, but I am too happy right now to worry about it.

His deep, boisterous laugh only makes me smile more. "You look like a drowned cat."

I gasp, affronted. "You're one to talk. You have a beard made of sand."

Jonathan turns his face slowly back and forth, showing off his sand-ridden face. "I rather think it makes me look dashing."

My heart seizes for a moment. He does look dashing and handsome.

He is a wonderful man, and he is everything my heart should desire.

So why doesn't it?

Why is the spot where Jonathan should be still hollow? It feels like the hole is shaped for something other than a life with this man. With any man, really.

I give him a small smile. "You are, indeed, an extremely dashing man, Jonathan." He hooks his finger under my chin and places a soft kiss on my lips. He tastes of sea salt mixed with the bite of coffee. While the kiss is sweet and sends a flood of heat to my core, I know now that this is not the path I must walk.

He pulls away and looks at me with adoration that twists my insides with guilt. "Let's get you home and into dry clothes."

We sit in the back of a carriage in silence. He holds my hand and gently brushes his thumb across the back of it. How can I break this man's heart? I care for him, truly I do. If the circumstances were different, we would fit perfectly together.

But that is not the case. He is not my destiny.

A thump forms in my throat and I swallow it down, determined not to cry.

It is the longest carriage ride of my life.

When we finally arrive at my apartment, my legs feel like lead as we ascend the stairs to my door. I have been agonizing over my words since we departed from the beach, and nothing seems right. There is nothing I can say that will remove the sting from what I am about to do.

"I had an amazing time today, Elsie."

"I did, too." My voice cracks. Jonathan's brow furrows with concern, and his blue eyes cloud grey with worry.

"What troubles you? Is it something I have done?" He cups the side of my face, and I lean into his touch despite myself.

"No," I whisper, hoarse with emotion. "No," I repeat with more clarity. "Jonathan, I must be honest with you as much as it pains me to do so. I care for you. You are truly wonderful, and I am so happy to know you, but this life that you want…that you *deserve*…" I pause, trying to find the right words. "It is not my dream."

His face falls, and his hand drops from my face. The loss of contact is like a fissure in the earth, and Jonathan and I are on opposite sides, growing further and further apart by the moment.

"El, I do not understand. What are you saying?"

"I am sorry, Jonathan. There is this yearning within me that thirsts for a life beyond Brooklyn, beyond settling down. It would be unfair to continue as we are."

He shakes his head and rakes his hands through his hair, sending sand cascading down on his shoulders. "I do not know what to say. I thought we had something special."

I take his hand in mine, and he flinches but does not entirely pull away. "*You* are special, and I will cherish our time together." I squeeze his hand, and a tear falls down my cheek, leaving a sticky trail on my salty skin.

He raises my hand to kiss my knuckles, looking at me wistfully. "Thank you for your candor, El. I hope you find what it is you are looking for."

I hug Jonathan, and he returns the embrace, inhaling the scent of my hair. "Take care of yourself, Jonathan. May you find every happiness in this life and beyond." I extract myself from his arms and hurry to my apartment with a heavy heart.

SCENE ELEVEN

BROOKLYN

"OH, EL. THAT SOUNDS positively horrible."

I take a long swig from the bottle of hooch I proffered from Teddy a few days ago at the market. Recoiling at its overwhelming taste, I smack my lips, then drink down another gulp before passing it to Nora.

The air is thick with humidity, even at this late hour. Nora and I sit on the fire escape outside my window in various states of undress, desperate for the tiniest relief from the oppressive summer heat.

Nora sniffs the bottle tentatively before taking a sip. "Blech!" She almost spits the cheap swill out. A bit dribbles down her chin, and she wipes it with the back of her hand. "El! How d'ye drink this? It's terrible."

"Give it here!"

She moves the bottle out of my reach. "I didn't say I didn't want it." Her words are clipped with the cadence of her accent. She takes a longer pull and sucks air through her teeth. "Whew!"

I snatch the bottle back. "It *was* horrible." I take another sip. "Nora. Do you think there is something the matter with me? He is kind and funny, and I just..." I trail off.

How do I explain to Nora that the reason I cannot be with Jonathan is because of her? How do I explain that my life is bound to hers? That we are destined to live the life we were robbed of all those centuries ago?

I take another gulp of liquid courage and let the bottle dangle between my legs as I sit with my knees pulled to my chest. "Do you ever feel like this life wasn't built for you?"

"In what way?"

I lean my head back against the rough brick and look up at the clear sky. "We are expected to marry and raise children and just accept a stationary life. What if there was another way?" I push myself forward and kneel facing Nora. "What if we forged our own path?"

She studies my face. My lantern illuminates her face against the dark of the alley between our building and the one across the way. The corner of her mouth ticks up just a little. She presses a finger to my nose.

"Your cheeks still grow pink with drink, cara mia."

She quickly pulls her hand away from my face as I stare at her, stunned by the observation and that Italian term of endearment.

Cara mia. Her dear.

Hers.

I say nothing as Nora puzzles over her words, giving her space to work through them. She laughs nervously. "I don't know why I said that. How would I know that?"

Silently, I stare back, communicating my feelings with my eyes, encouraging her.

"It's preposterous, right? El?"

"Is it truly that unbelievable?" I respond gently. Setting down the bottle, I twine my fingers with hers. Her heart is galloping, eyes wide with disbelief.

Grasping at her heart, Nora is practically thrown back against the building by an invisible force. Golden light emits from her chest and coils in swirls to connect with my own. The light works its way into my heart, my soul, stitching itself into place.

The relief is instantaneous. The part of me that always felt empty, always searching for its missing piece, thrums happily.

"Chiara?" My name comes out of her mouth as a gasp of surprise.

Biting my lip, I nod. "Welcome back, ma sorella."

Her hands fly to her mouth, muffling her strangled sob.

She is on me in an instant, drawing me into a fierce hug. Her arms are shaking, and she whispers into my hair over and over. "Chiara. Oh, my sister. My dear sister. I found you."

I laugh through my own tears. "You did. You did find me."

She smacks my arm. "Did ye know this whole time? And ye didn't tell me?"

I shrink back sheepishly. "Would you have believed me? Some crazy woman on a pier saying, 'Welcome to New York. I'm your sister from three hundred years ago?' You would have taken the next ship back to Ireland."

Marcella crosses her arms and looks down her nose at me, shaking her head. "You are the menace you have always been, Chiara."

I push my bottom lip out and pout. "Ninety-one years and I have you back for three minutes, and you are already scolding me." I cannot even pretend to be angry. We are both cackling with laughter, heads bent together.

The heat suddenly doesn't seem so oppressive as we huddle together, and I rest my head on her shoulder. "What do we do now?" I ask.

I bask in the comfort of the rise and fall of Marcella's breathing while she ponders my question.

"I have an idea."

SCENE TWELVE

BROOKLYN

AUGUST 1887

I STAND AT GRAND Central Depot with my valise and satchel among people milling about the train depot, ready to depart for their destinations. Checking my pocket watch for the fifth time in as many minutes, nervous thoughts dance at the edge of my mind that she has changed her mind. The summer heat has large beads of sweat sluicing down my back, but I am too anxious to care.

After Marcella regained her memories, we spent the last two months scraping together as much savings as we could manage, working ourselves to the bone at our jobs, and taking on any odd jobs offered by our neighbors. Teddy pitched in as well, helping us sell our furniture and other possessions that would not be practical to keep. It was exhausting, but worth it because we finally have enough money to leave New York.

Leaving Teddy behind is the only truly difficult part of leaving, for both Marcella and me. I love Teddy as I do my own family and he and Nora developed a special friendship of their own in their short time together. And as close as Teddy and I are, I think he is perhaps a little more broken up over losing his chance with "Nora" than losing me.

In our limited free hours, Marcella and I wrote in my dream journal, filling in the gaps in my knowledge of our lives as Georgette and Audrey, then as Kat and Odette. Marcella filled page after page with the secrets of her life, her feelings, and her own dreams as the memories continued to come back to her.

We wrote of magic, recreating the grimoires of the families I have been gifted over the centuries, and those Marcella has known as well.

Our books, our words hold power all their own. We defied the will of man. When men demanded we submit, that we abandon our free will for their whims and egos, Marcella and I persisted.

And in our persistence, we were reborn.

I check my watch once more and bounce on the balls of my feet. Where is she?

As I tuck a stray curl up into my cap to keep it off my neck, I feel the familiar and comforting tug in my chest and know that Marcella is near. Before she says a word, I feel her sidle up to me. We stand next to one another, studying the train schedule before us. I look to my left and am stunned at her appearance. Gone is the prim attire and neatly pinned-back hair. Marcella wears her waves free with a scarf tied around her head to keep her hair off her forehead. She is donning trousers and one of my sleeveless blouses, tailored to include new pearl buttons.

Her grin is wide and bright. "Where to, sister?"

I take her hand and pick up my valise with my other. "Everywhere."

ACT FIVE

PITTSBURGH, PENNSYLVANIA

MARCH 1999

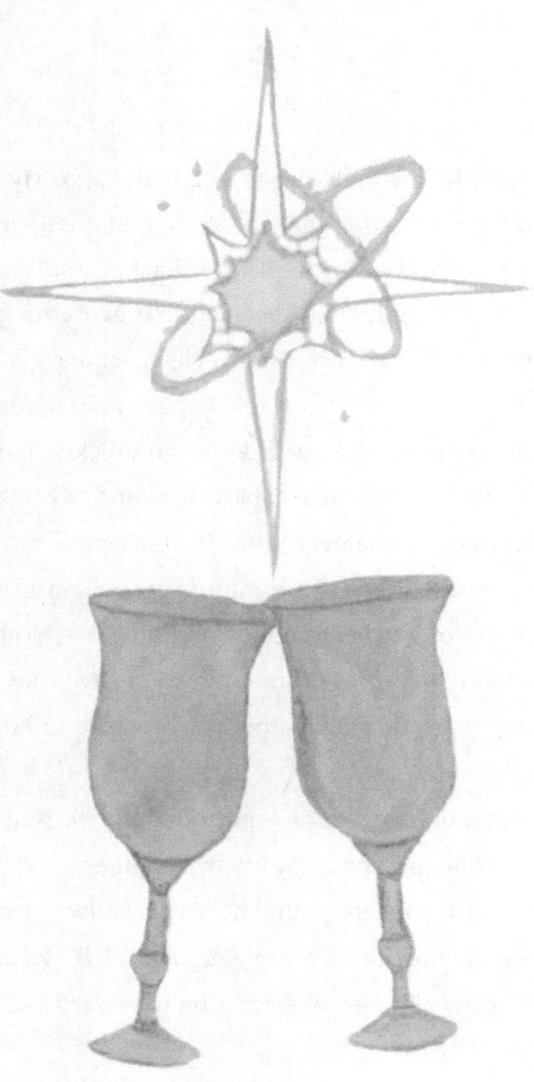

SCENE ONE

PITTSBURGH

THE SHARP PAIN IN my belly began two hours ago. My water has not broken yet, and the contractions are about ten minutes apart. I have time.

My bag has been packed for weeks, but Rachel is still rushing around our apartment, double and triple-checking that everything is ready and perfect for delivery. She has been my rock, coaching me through each contraction, but I still have not been able to get a hold of Matteo.

You'd think I would want my labor to go quickly, but I don't want Matteo to miss this. They're his babies, too, and we want him to be involved in their lives in whatever capacity he wishes.

He's been my best friend since middle school, so if he thought he was ever getting rid of me, being mine and Rachel's sperm donor sealed his fate. I have too much dirt on him anyway. I saved my mom's home videos of our eighth-grade talent show performance to *Wham!* and I am not afraid to use it.

Another contraction comes on, spasming and seizing so much this time that I cry out and grab onto the kitchen counter for support.

"Holly!" Rachel's footsteps pound down the hallway from the nursery into our kitchenette. She looks completely frazzled. Her auburn hair is falling out of the claw clip, her sweater is on backwards, and her eyeliner is smudged across her face.

I breathe through the contraction while Rachel rubs my lower back. "Inhale, love." She sucks in a breath through her nose, and I try to mimic the rhythm of her breathing, but my pain is quickly replaced by the feel of liquid running down my leg and a splash on the tile floor. My eyes fly up to meet hers. I watch her expression quickly change from alarm to pure joy.

"Time to go, momma." She leans in and kisses me tenderly. Just as I fall into the kiss, her lips are ripped from mine. I groan. "Come on! Let's get your shoes on."

She puts her arm around me and leads me toward the door. "Rachel, slow down! I can't go like this!" I gesture to my wet pajama shorts. "And can we talk for a second about your appearance?"

Her face screws up in shock. "Is now the time?"

I laugh and kiss her cheek. "Just go check the mirror. I'm going to change and get my bag."

Waddling uncomfortably to our bedroom, my mind races at a million miles per hour with what I assume are typical new mom fears about the babies and their health and happiness, and one other nagging thought about the fact that we still have not chosen names.

Rachel insists we will know their names when we meet them, but what if we can't agree on them? What if we choose names, but we didn't think of all the cruel nicknames other kids may come up with? What if Matteo doesn't like the names? Should he even have a say? Will he be mad if he isn't included in the naming? Why didn't we think about this before? Oh my Go—

"Owww! Ow, ow, ow!" I suck air in through my teeth, and Rachel is back again, this time with her sweater only partially on, as she was likely just trying to twist it around.

"Holly, we need to go, unless you plan on delivering in our living room."

Those words awaken an entirely new fear, prompting me to move a little faster. "I am *not* delivering these babies at home like a dog!"

She finds me clean clothes and helps me undress and redress in sweatpants, clean panties, and a sweatshirt. She slips my swollen feet into my checkered Vans that are a size too big and escorts me to the door, grabbing my overnight bag on the way out. I've never been so grateful to live on the first floor. If I had to walk down stairs right now, I'm afraid I would just roll down like a watermelon.

Once I am strapped into the passenger seat of Rachel's Toyota Camry, I fumble with the CDs in the visor to find the mix I made for the drive to the hospital. Bush "Machinehead" blares through the car speakers.

"Really, Holly? This is what you chose? Nice blinker, asshole!" Rachel swerves around a car that cut her off, and I grab the handle above my window dramatically.

"Um, sweetheart, can we please not shake the babies out of me? And yes. I thought this would be good driving music for you. That was my misTAKE! Aaaaargh!" Another contraction seizes my belly. "Drive faster! Drive faster!" I command through my labored breaths.

The rest of the short ride to Magee Women's Hospital from our apartment in the Shady Side neighborhood of Pittsburgh is relatively smooth. Rachel only gave two other drivers the finger and blew through one stop sign. Once we arrive, the nurses get me checked in while Rachel parks the car. They're taking my vitals when Rachel finds me. She calmly explains our special situation, and the nurse is wonderfully supportive.

Rachel's soft lips press to my sweaty forehead, and she brushes my hair back. "You're doing great, love. I'm going to call Matteo again. I'll be right back."

"Okay. Hurry!"

"We're actually ready to take her up to a room. You can call from there."

SCENE TWO

PITTSBURGH

"COME ON, MATTEO. PICK up! Hey, Matteo. It's Rachel," she says to his answering machine. "We're at the hospital. Come straight here. Do not pass *Go*. Do Not Collect Two Hundred Dollars. Babies are coming *now*. Bye."

I groan and bite back my tears. Where is he? I don't want him to miss this.

"Did I miss it?" As if summoned by my thoughts, Matteo breezes into the room, holding a stuffed bear, balloons, and a bouquet of daisies. He shoves them all at Rachel and rushes to my bedside. "Oh, honey. You look… radiant."

He gently pats my shoulder, cringing at my disheveled appearance. He looks immaculate in loose jeans, a tight-fitting shirt, and a leather jacket. An earring with a cross dangles from his right ear, his dark brown hair is perfectly styled like Brad Pitt's, and I seriously cannot believe he showed up looking ready to hit East Carson Street for drinks.

I rest my hands on my bulging belly and give him a pointed look. "Hey, babies," he croons, as he leans down and kisses my belly, and I smack his head. "Ouch! What?"

"Why are you dressed like that?"

He straightens and runs a hand through his hair. "What? First impressions are important. And I need to set a standard of good fashion for these children, because their mother is a lost cause." Matteo glances over his shoulder at Rachel, who is standing helplessly with the armload of gifts. "Not you, Rach. Great sweater choice."

"It was backwards an hour ago," I grumble under my breath. I'm relieved when Dr. Francis enters, her stilettos clicking across the floor. A nurse is right behind her.

"Matteo, you must work on your bedside manner," Dr. Francis chides. "How's momma doing?"

"I'd like the drugs, please," I smile sweetly and bat my eyelashes for good measure. "Or for you to forcibly remove Matteo. I will settle for either."

Dr. Francis chuckles and snaps on a pair of gloves. "Matteo, can you alleviate Rachel of that wonderful armful of gifts so that she can stand with Holly for the exam? Melissa, get the curtain, please?"

I love Dr. Francis. She commands a room, but does so in a way that makes you feel important. The nurse, Melissa, closes the curtain by the door with *shuuush* to grant me some privacy, then joins Dr. Francis.

"Yes, ma'am."

"Matteo, stop being a kiss ass," Rachel chastises.

My friend's face falls, and I can see the remorse in his eyes for not reading the room appropriately. I'm not mad at him. This is new territory for all of us, and I know he is just as scared as Rachel and I are of being parents.

While Matteo will not be moving in with us, he will be involved. We haven't defined terms— we're just going to take things day by day and let him develop his own relationship with the babies.

We used both of our eggs for fertilization, so there is a really good chance that the babies could be biologically mine and my partner's. Our own family— just like we've always dreamed.

"Is there anything Holly can have to be more comfortable?" Matteo asks the nurse, who smiles kindly at him.

"Yes, she can have ice chips. They can get them for you at the nurse's station. Down the hall to the left."

Matteo quietly slips from the room, and Dr. Francis begins her exam, talking me through every step. "Well, Holly. You're advancing really quickly. I'm sorry, but the window for the epidural has passed."

Maybe I don't like Dr. Francis as much as I thought. I try to sit up. "What do you mean?" I squeak out, panicked. My birth plan has gone completely out the window. "Rachel, what does she mean?" I grip her hand, and she grits her teeth but doesn't let go, even though I'm probably crushing her bones with my death grip.

"Dr. Francis, are there no other options?" Rachel asks.

She gives us a sympathetic smile. "I'm afraid not. It's time to go to the delivery room. Your babies are coming. I'm going to go scrub in, and I'll meet you there. Melissa, grab Lindsay and take Holly to delivery."

I want to sob. I want to scream. I want to run out of the room. I'm not ready for this. What was I thinking? I'm not just having *one* baby. I'm having *two* with no pain management, and I haven't even listened to my birthing mixed CD all the way through. I don't have names. I don't even know if they are boys or girls or one of each. Why didn't we find out? Why didn't we get a bigger car? Two car seats? I don't want a minivan.

My mental spiral is cut short by another contraction, and I cannot stop the wail that tears from my throat. Rachel squeezes my hand back and talks me through the breathing. The building pressure between my legs is about to give.

"Rachel, I think I need to push."

Her face goes pale. The nurses are running around us, preparing to wheel me to the delivery room. Matteo comes in to find the room in utter chaos, holding two cups of ice chips.

"Matteo, it's time for Holly to go to delivery. Melissa, is he allowed to be in the room with us to help coach?" Rachel asks.

"Of course. Holly, we're going to start moving you down the hall now. You *must not* push until we are there, okay? Can you do that for me?"

I nod, not feeling at all confident that these babies aren't about to shoot out of me like cannonballs. I try to close my legs, but to no avail.

Another nurse raises the railings on the bed and starts wheeling me out of the room. The fear dissipates and turns into something different—something new that I have not felt before. My stomach warms, and it is an odd feeling, but not unpleasant. A wave of calm crashes over me, traveling through my body and settling in my heart.

I can't explain it, but I know with everything that I am that something important is about to happen. Something that was destined.

SCENE THREE

PITTSBURGH

I'VE BEEN PUSHING FOR what feels like an eternity. Rachel and Matteo's arms are hooked around my legs, and any modesty I've ever felt in my life has flown right out of the window.

"Ready to go again? You can do this, Holly. One, two, three," Dr. Francis counts out, and I bear down with all my might. "Four, five… I see a head, keep going, Holly. You're almost there."

I scream and keep pushing through the intense burning sensation. My teeth grind together as I keep pushing through the ten count. At nine, I am flooded with relief and flop backward as the first baby emerges.

Dr. Francis's triumphant voice announces, "It's a girl!"

"Oh, she is beautiful, Holly," Rachel breathes. I try to sit up and watch as Rachel tearfully cuts her umbilical cord. Dr. Francis holds the wailing child up so I can see her, then hands her off to a nurse. She is so tiny and has little wisps of blonde hair, like me.

"She looks just like you. Especially the screaming," Matteo cracks, and kisses my cheek.

I choke out a laugh between sobs and lie back, panting.

Dr. Francis's smile fades, and she is right back to business. "Okay, Holly. The next baby is coming. Let's go again. One big push and you're all done, momma." Melissa approaches and whispers something in the doctor's ear. Her brow furrows, but she turns her full attention back to me.

Panic surges through me like a bolt of lightening. "What? What's wrong? Is she okay? Is my daughter okay?"

"Doctor, is the baby alright?" Matteo inquires. Rachel's hand is shaking in my own.

"Yes, she's okay. Rachel, get Holly's leg. Let's go on three. Three, two, one, push."

Matteo helps me sit upright, and I try not to think about whatever the nurse said and focus on pushing.

Rachel counts this time. "Five, six, seven—" The high-pitched cries of another baby cut off her counting. "Oh, Holly! It's another girl!" This time, Matteo steps forward as we previously agreed to cut her umbilical cord. Tears stream down his cheeks, and for just a singular moment, nothing else in the world matters but the family we have created.

The nurse quickly takes the baby away before I am able to see her. "Wait, where are you taking her? What aren't you telling us?" Rachel's shrill accusation makes my stomach plummet.

A mother's intuition is absolutely real. I am *feral*. "Dr. Francis, what's wrong? Tell me right now!" My forceful demand sounds meek and pathetic through my tears. I try to peer around her at the nurses tending to my daughters.

The puzzled look on her face does nothing to calm my nerves. Matteo is a blubbering mess, and Rachel looks ready to rush the nurses, but she stays by my side. "As far as I know, your daughters are perfectly healthy. There is an…anomaly. They have scars on their chests. They're identical."

"Scars? *How?* They were just born! Let me see them!" I shriek so loudly I can probably be heard throughout the hospital.

"Please, Holly. I need you to lie back so I can deliver the placenta. We will bring them to you shortly and then take them to run some tests. Their vitals are good. It's a good sign. We have already paged the on-call pediatrician."

I don't know what else to do. I just nod and lie back on the pillows. Rachel's delicate hands wipe the moisture from my cheeks. "Hey, it's going to be fine. I'm so proud of you. You are the most incredible and strongest woman in the world. I love you." I look into my partner's pale green eyes, and though there is fear, there is also love and hope.

"I love you, too." Her soft lips brush against mine, and I taste the salt of her own tears on my lips.

A hushed voice speaks up behind Rachel. "I'm sorry to interrupt, but would the new mommies like to hold their daughters?" We separate, now laughing through our tears. I take Matteo's hand and squeeze it.

Melissa hands me baby number one, and another nurse hands Rachel baby number two. They are tightly swaddled in blankets. Matteo leans down over me to kiss our daughter's head, inhaling her sweet and soft scent. Her eyes are closed, and she is making cooing sounds. "I have never loved someone so much in my entire life," he whispers to her.

Her fine, blonde wisps of hair tickle my nose as I bring her to my face next to kiss her forehead. Rachel joins me on the bed, holding our other daughter, who has a thick head of dark hair, just like Matteo. She has Rachel's pouty mouth and nose.

Dr. Francis finishes up and removes her gloves. "Do these beauties have names yet?"

Rachel and I exchange a nervous and somewhat guilty glance for not having names. But something is prickling at me. I close my eyes for a moment and let the thought fully form.

"Chiara," I whisper.

Matteo nods his approval. "Strong Italian name."

I look at Rachel, and she smiles. "What about this little one?" She nuzzles our daughter's face with her nose.

"Marcella." The name is out of my mouth before I realize I've said it.

"Chiara and Marcella." Rachel tests the names. "They're perfect."

"Beautiful names. I'm going to go check in on my other patients. The nurses will finish up in here and get you back to your room. Pediatrics will take the girls to look them over. They will bring them right back to your room as soon as possible."

"Thank you, Doctor," I say.

"I'll come check on you tomorrow, Holly. Congratulations to you all." She gives a wave and quietly leaves us.

Matteo waves a nurse over. "There is a camera in my jacket pocket over there. Can you please take a photo of us?"

She obliges and takes a few photos of all of us, and then just me and Rachel with the girls. A knock at the door disrupts the impromptu photo shoot. The head of a middle-aged man in a white jacket pops in.

"Good evening. I hear we have two little girls! Congratulations!" His salt and pepper hair is neatly combed back, and he has kind blue eyes. "I'm Dr. Winston, the on-call pediatrician."

I was so swept up in the emotion of holding Chiara for the first time that I completely forgot about the marks on their skin. How could I forget something like that? Am I already failing at being a mother?

Melissa briefs Dr. Winston, and I cannot stop the protective hold I have on Chiara. I'm afraid to look under the blanket to see what marks her tender skin. The energy in the room has noticeably shifted. Matteo and Rachel both stiffen on either side of me. The only sounds I hear are the soft breaths of my daughters and the beating of my own heart in my ears.

I study Dr. Winston's expression and body language as Melissa relays the details of the birth and describes the anomalies on Marcella and Chiara's chests. He remains stoic, nodding along. "Well." He claps his hands. "Let's take a peek and see what we have." He gestures to Rachel first. "May I?"

Rachel hands over Marcella, but tears are silently falling down her face.

"Here," I offer. "You haven't held Chiara yet."

"Thank you, love." I carefully shift Chiara to her arms, immediately missing her in a way I didn't think was possible. She is right next to me, in the arms of her mother, but her absence is like a deep well that has no bottom. It takes all of my restraint not to snatch our daughter back from

Rachel or to touch her, but my partner needs this time to bond without my interference.

A nurse wheels over a bassinet for Dr. Winston to place Marcella in. "What is this precious little girl's name?" He is bouncing her lightly in his arms. His demeanor puts me slightly more at ease, as he clearly loves his job and has a good temperament for dealing with both children and stressed-out parents.

"Marcella," Matteo responds.

"Welcome to the world, Marcella. Let's see what we have. Oh, yes, I know it's a little cold, isn't it?" Marcella fusses as he peels back the blanket, and it cracks my heart in two to hear her in distress. "Hmmm. Quite remarkable." He runs a finger over her chest, and I sit up, craning my neck, desperate to see what he sees.

"Can I see?" I ask.

"Of course. Melissa, can you please give Marcella to Holly and bring me her sister?"

The nurse lays Marcella in my lap. Right over her heart is a scar in the shape of an eight-pointed star. Hesitantly, my hand moves to touch it. The raised skin is smooth and pink against her olive complexion and warm to the touch.

It isn't ugly or obtrusive. The star is a part of her that just… fits.

"Wow," Rachel softly breathes.

"Is it too late to change her name to Stellina?" Matteo asks, awestruck. "It means 'star' in Italian," he clarifies our confused looks.

Dr. Winston places Chiara next to her sister, and we take in the identical starbursts. "What would you call her then?" He asks, a half-smile playing at his lips.

"Stellina Junior." Matteo looks dead serious, but I know him. He loses his battle to keep his laugh in.

I smack his arm and turn my attention back to the girls. "Dr. Winston, do you know what has caused this?"

Running a hand through his hair, he scratches at the back of his head. "I can honestly say this is a real puzzler, but at a cursory look, they seem perfectly healthy. I don't hear any distress in their heartbeats or breathing, but I will still need to run some tests."

Before any of us can ask what tests he is planning, he continues. "I'll start with blood panels to rule out any potential genetic abnormalities before doing anything more intrusive. We'll take this one step at a time." His pager goes off. "I need to check in on another patient, but worry not. We'll get this figured out. I'm going to have the nurses bring the girls to the nursery and get you settled in your room. I'll have them back to you as soon as possible." He checks his watch. "Melissa, can you please make sure dinner service is delivered to Holly?"

"Of course."

He affectionately pats each girl on her head and leaves us.

Nurses prepare to take all of us to our next destinations, but they do not exist to me. I cannot pull my eyes from these two perfect beings. As if on instinct, they snuggle into one another, craving the comfort of the sister they shared a womb with for the last nine months. I don't know if it is a trick of the light or my exhaustion, but a soft halo of gold light surrounds Marcella and Chiara, as if insulating them in their own bubble where only the two of them exist.

SCENE FOUR

PITTSBURGH

MY DAUGHTERS ARE GIVEN a clean bill of health. Testing revealed nothing out of the ordinary. It seems that my little stars are blessed by some other invisible force of nature.

Settling into motherhood has been the biggest challenge of my life. I am hoping to breastfeed for as long as I can, but sleep is not coming easily, as I have to feed both girls. Rachel wakes up with me every time, taking the girls for diaper changes after their late-night feedings so that I can go back to sleep.

I know she is exhausted, too. The purple circles under our eyes are hard-earned, but we've never been happier. Rachel took vacation from her teaching job for the first few weeks, but has been back at work for a month now. Matteo relieves us after dinner most nights— which we have not had to cook for weeks. His mother has our fridge overflowing with pasta, lasagna, soup, and homemade bread. I begged him to bring us fruits and vegetables after the first week of all carbs. I do appreciate how supportive and hands-on she is, though.

My mom helps on weekends, and Rachel's sister, Tracy, stops by whenever she can with her two children. Our niece and nephew are completely enamored with the twins, lying on the floor with the girls on their play mat, tickling their bellies and singing songs from *Sesame Street.*

Rachel's parents have not been accepting of our relationship at all, and even less so of our decision to have children. Though I remind her that it is their loss, I know how much it hurts her to not have her family around. I hope one day they wake up and realize that the only thing that matters is Rachel's happiness and that they have two healthy, beautiful granddaughters.

Marcella and Chiara, even at two months old, have formed distinct personalities. Marcella is our serene child, sleeping peacefully through the night and even-tempered during the day. Chiara, on the other hand... I think I found my first grey hair. She is strong-willed and loudly proclaims her displeasure with even the mildest discomfort.

I keep teasing Rachel that she gets that from her, but she isn't having it since it is completely evident, even without genetic testing, that Chiara is biologically my daughter and Marcella is hers.

Which leaves her fussy temperament likely to be inherited from Matteo, and I am completely fine needling him with this theory every time he is around.

I've come to calling her Star Fire. It fits her. She is an inferno that will command respect. Marcella is my Starlight— my quiet soul, who will be the North Star for those around her.

June greets us with two straight weeks of rain before the solstice, which brings unbearable humidity. My two little Pisces are happiest in their Aunt Tracy's pool, splashing their feet and floating around in their baby rafts.

Rachel's sister bought them heart-shaped sunglasses, and they look absolutely adorable. Well, Marcella does. I swear, we could wrap that child like a mummy, and she would just chill and take it. Chiara fussed until the sunglasses fell from her face and sank to the bottom of the pool.

When the girls are finally down for the night, I collapse onto the couch next to Rachel. Her nose and cheeks are red from our day at Tracy's house, and despite how tired and sunburned she is, she looks gorgeous. Our apartment is hot and sticky, but I don't care. I pull her into me and kiss the crown of her head. A low moan rumbles in her throat.

"Holly, it is five million degrees," she murmurs, half asleep. Her auburn hair blows around from the standing fan that she has aimed directly at our faces, tickling my nose.

"I don't care. Our daughters are miraculously both asleep. I want to hold my girlfriend."

She cracks an eye and looks up at me through the strands of hair that are slicked across her damp forehead. "I'll allow it. Play with my hair." She slides down so her head is in my lap, kicking her legs over the side of the couch. "Mmmm...that feels good," she sighs as I run my fingers through her hair.

Her normally smooth hair is frizzed from the humidity. I gently untangle it with my fingers, massaging her scalp as I go. I bite my lip as she happily moans again, and heat stirs in my belly. She is sprawled in my lap in nothing but a camisole and her panties, and I can't think of anything in the world I want more than to be with her right now. Heat be damned.

"You know what else would feel good?" I coyly ask.

She cracks her eye once more. "Oh yeah?"

I nod. "Yeah, but slow." It will be our first time since I was medically cleared for sex.

She sits up and pulls her camisole over her head, tossing it aside. "Finally, an excuse to not wear clothes in this heat." Laughing, she climbs onto my lap and captures my mouth with her own.

We make love right there, and it's unhurried, like we have all the time in the world in this bubble that is just the two of us. I savor the taste of Rachel and the feel of her soft skin against my own for what feels like the first time. We've fallen into motherhood headfirst, but we need to start remembering to make space for us.

Rachel and I fall asleep on the couch, tangled together, our breathing and hearts synced so that there is no differentiating where one of us ends and the other begins.

I didn't think a heart could feel this full, but I have everything in the world I've ever needed or wanted under this roof. My every happiness has manifested itself in the family we've created.

As I'm drifting to sleep, Chiara's high pitched wail sounds from down the hall like a little siren. "Stay here, mama. I'll get her." Rachel kisses my cheek and extracts herself from my arms to get our daughter to bring her to me to feed.

All I can do is smile as I watch her stumble down the hall as she tries to pull her tank top back over her head.

SCENE FIVE

PITTSBURGH

OCTOBER 2005

"UNCLE TEO!" CHIARA THROWS herself at Matteo before he is fully through the door of our house.

He doubles over a bit, and I know she knocked the wind out of him. "Hi, Kiki," he rasps, then recovers and hugs her fiercely. She squeals as he picks her up and swings her in a circle. When she's returned to the ground, he leans in like he has a secret. "Make sure you give Uncle Rob the same exact hug. Got it?"

"What type of hug?" A deep, booming voice asks from the porch. With a mischievous glint in her blue eyes, Chiara launches herself at Matteo's partner, Rob.

"Oof! Hey, little dynamite!"

"Uncle Rob, did you see I lost *two* whole teeth?" She holds up her fingers and then opens her mouth wide, showing off her missing front teeth.

"My girl!" He offers her a high-five, which she enthusiastically slaps. "What did the tooth fairy bring?"

"The tooth fairy brought me two dollars!"

"Two dollars! What are you buying me?" Rob asks, trying to hide his smile.

Chiara puts her hands on her hips and looks up at him accusingly. "I lost *my* teeth. You have to give *me* money."

Before I can chastise her for her manners, Marcella comes bounding into the room, wearing her coat and a Hello Kitty backpack. "Uncle Teo! I lost one tooth!"

"Holly, how much money are they going to take me for this weekend?" He pulls Marcella into a hug and gives me a pointed look.

"All of it!" Chiara screams and falls over laughing. My wild child's hair is falling out of its ponytail, and she only has one shoe on. There are no fewer than five star stickers strewn about her face.

I weave my way around the girls to hug Matteo and Rob. "One dollar each, no more than that, please," I whisper in Rob's ear. "Do not let him go overboard."

He scoffs. "Do you really think I can stop him?" Rob towers over me. He is over six feet tall and pure muscle, with hazel eyes that pop in contrast to his rich brown skin. It's easy to see why Matteo is so enamored with him. Plus, he is incredibly supportive of our unique family dynamic, treating the girls like he would his own daughters. The twins absolutely adore him.

Rachel pops her head in from the kitchen. "Rob, one of you needs to be the adult, and we know it won't be Teo." She quirks an eyebrow, then gives Matteo an "eyes on you" gesture.

My best friend makes a face at Rachel and returns his attention to Marcella.

"Chells Bells, what do you say we eat *all* the ice cream and candy we can before I bring you and your sister home tomorrow? Your mommies will *love* it!"

Marcella glances at me, then at Rachel, who is calmly observing from the kitchen doorway. "Momma and Mommy don't let us have that much candy. We'll get belly aches and cavalries."

"Ha!" Rachel raises her arms triumphantly.

"You mean cavities, Starlight."

Her little face scrunches up. "That's what I said. Cavalries."

I gently boop her nose with my finger and smile. "So you did, little

Starlight. Give me a hug, then go hug Momma. I need to get your sister ready to go." I kneel so Marcella can wrap her little arms around me, and I breathe in her soft scent.

Wrangling Chiara into her coat and her other shoe is an adventure, but one I am at least well attuned to at this point. She marches to the beat of her own drum so much so that I think there is literally a drum in her head that she is constantly dancing to. I wouldn't have her any other way.

I watch the girls as they walk down the driveway to Matteo's car. They hold each other's hands tightly, and the glowing halo of gold around them is all I need to see to know they are happy.

I don't know if it is because they are twins or if it is the stars that mark them, but my girls have a relationship unlike any I've ever witnessed before. Marcella has a quiet way of tempering Chiara's feisty nature while still allowing her sister to be exactly who she is. Chiara pushes Marcella outside of her comfort zone, bolstering her to be brave because she will never let her sister fall alone.

Day by day, I watch them grow into their own people, but they also grow together.

SCENE SIX

PITTSBURGH

MARCH 20, 2012

"HOW ARE WE MOTHERS of thirteen-year-olds? I'm not even an adult yet." I bury my head in Rachel's shoulder and pull the quilt over my head. "I refuse to accept this." My voice is muffled, and the quilt is absorbing my tears.

Rachel shimmies down to join me under the blanket and places a quick kiss on my nose. The early morning light filters through the blankets. I'm always amazed by how ethereal Rachel looks in the morning, even more so with the amber light shining around her.

"I know," she sighs. "They're going to start high school soon, then comes driving."

A strained sob catches in my throat. "Why would you say that to me when I'm like this?" Tears come in waves that I cannot stop. Rachel hugs me to her.

"Oh, love. I didn't mean to make it worse." She strokes my hair and lets me cry under the safety of our bedding until I hear footsteps pounding down the hall.

"Oh, ew! You aren't like… doing it, are you? It's my birthday. That's child abuse!"

I huff a laugh through my tears, and we emerge from our cocoon, finding Chiara at the foot of our bed. "No. Mommy is just having a little bit of a hard time this morning. Come on over here, birthday girl." I see the glimmer of tears in Rachel's own eyes, even though she's trying to be strong for my sake.

Chiara is already dressed for school in jeans, *UGG* boots, and a Fall Out Boy T-shirt. There is what I assume to be an entire container of glitter on her face and *Silly Bandz* up her arms. Her strawberry-blonde hair is in a messy bun, but she is also wearing a rainbow glittering headband. She flops down next to me and takes my cheeks in her hands, smooshing them together.

"You know what will make you feel better, Mommy? If you made me pancakes."

"Mommy is crying, and you're asking for breakfast?" Marcella wanders in, looking more put together than her sister in jeans and a green sweater. Her chestnut hair is neatly brushed and hangs down on either side of her face, which is wrinkled with concern.

Chiara glares at her sister. "She can't *cry* if she's making pancakes, Chelly. I'm *helping*."

Marcella crawls onto the bed and shoves her sister out of the way, throwing her arms around me. "Thank you, Starlight. Happy birthday." Chiara coughs loudly. "Happy birthday, Star Fire. You are both so special."

Rachel wraps her arms around Marcella and me. "Get in here, Kiki. Family hug."

Chiara launches herself across the three of us, and I revel in being quite literally crushed by the love of my family. We stay there for a few moments, just existing in our own bubble.

In true Chiara fashion, she pulls us back to reality. "I love you all, and this is great, but where do we stand on the pancakes?" Rachel ruffles her hair, making our daughter screech.

"I know Mommy already said it, but we do love you more than we can ever begin to tell you. Go get your backpacks together, and I'll meet you in the kitchen." Rachel shoos the girls from our room and tosses the blanket back over our heads, kissing me deeply in our own world. "And I love you," she whispers against my lips.

I press my forehead to hers, closing my eyes and committing this moment of my life to memory. "I love you."

"Momma! Pancakes?"

Heads bent together, we shake with laughter, holding onto each other for just a moment longer before we begin our day.

SCENE SEVEN

PITTSBURGH

FOR THEIR BIRTHDAY, THE girls wanted to get pizza at *Fiori's* and go to their favorite vintage store to go "treasure hunting." Matteo and Rob meet us for pizza, doting on the girls and going completely overboard on clothes, headbands, and costume jewelry from *Claire's* for Chiara, and more clothes and books for Marcella.

Rachel and I had promised that for their birthday, they could get their ears pierced, which we plan to do over the weekend. Chiara tried to push for a tattoo, causing Rachel to turn pale as a ghost.

During dinner, I notice both girls fussing at their chests. "What's wrong with you two? Why are you rubbing at your scars?" I try my best to hide my concern, but after thirteen years of fretting that something would eventually show up as a result of their unusual scars, my panic is winning out.

Marcella squints and chews on her lip as she rubs at it. "I don't know. It's like… I dunno. It feels like it's throbbing or something."

"Yeah. It's weird." Chiara rubs at hers with one hand and shoves pizza into her mouth with her other, slightly less perturbed by the discomfort than her sister while she's in the presence of food.

"What do you mean 'throbbing?' Does it hurt? Is it red or swollen?" Matteo holds my gaze as he questions the girls.

They look at each other, then peer down their shirts. "No. It looks the same as always," Chiara reports from inside her shirt, mouth still full of pizza. "Can I get a new bra?" She pops out of her shirt. "Like neon green?"

Rachel puts her arm around our daughter and pulls her into a side hug. "Your mind never ceases to amaze me, kiddo."

I shake my head and smile a little. It makes me feel a little better that the girls aren't distressed, but I can't let this go. "Well, I'd feel better if we went to the doctor to get it checked out, just in case."

Their faces fall. "Mooooom! We're supposed to go to the shop!" Chiara wails.

"I know, I know. We are still going. I'll call the doctor in the morning and get you an appointment. We won't go now. But if it gets worse, you need to tell us, and we're going straight to the ER."

Chiara immediately removes her hand from her chest. "It's fine. Nothing is wrong. Can I have a quarter? I want a gumball." She stands from her seat, then adds, "Two quarters. One for Chelly, too."

Rob fishes money from his pocket and gives my daughter a fistful of change. "Thanks, Uncle Rob!" She kisses his cheek, then drags her sister to the candy machines by the door.

An hour later, I'm slightly calmer as we browse around the labyrinth of antiques and trinkets at the shop. Rachel and I are picking through old jewelry while the girls go off on their own adventure in search of their hearts' desires.

The store is getting ready to close, and Chiara is still rooting around for the perfect item. Marcella is sitting in a rocking chair with her choices in her lap: a music box, a blue ceramic bowl, and a beaded necklace.

I search through the stacks of items for her sister and find her standing in the middle of an aisle looking lost. "Hey there, Star Fire. They're closing soon. You about ready to go?"

She is chewing on her lip and bouncing on the balls of her feet. "Just five more minutes, Mommy. Please! There is something here that I need. I know it. I just… I just need to find it."

I look at her quizzically, but I don't question her further. I know my daughter, and when her heart is set on something, she will not give up until she gets it.

"Okay, five minutes. We need to get home. It's a school night. If you don't find anything today, we can come back another day."

Her brow is furrowed in concentration, and I know she hasn't heard a word I've said. She finally moves, disappearing around a corner and is back on the hunt. Two minutes later, she reappears, gleeful and shoving a tin box at me. It's locked, but it is beautiful, with its blue and silver floral embossing and slight patina to its edges. "This is it! I found it!"

She looks so proud of herself. "Then let's get it."

We arrive home, and her jacket is barely off before she takes Marcella's hand and drags her upstairs. "Come on!"

"Kiki! You're gonna pull my arm off!"

They thunder up the stairs, followed by the slamming of their bedroom door.

SCENE EIGHT

MARCH 20, 2012

MARCELLA

MY TWIN SISTER SHOVES me into our room and slams the door behind us. "Keeks! What are you doing?"

She locks the door and turns around, a huge smile on her face. "Sit." She plops down on the yellow daisy rug that's between our beds and starts prying at the lock on the tin box she got at the antique store. Grunting, she yanks at the lock. "Damn!"

"Kiki! Shhhhh! Our moms will hear you!"

She waves a hand at me. "Calm down, Swears Police. I didn't say the 'F' word." She turns the box over, and whatever is inside clutters around.

"Why don't you see if Momma has something in the garage that can cut it open?" I sit down and spread out my own items on the carpet to show her what I got, but she doesn't notice. She's too busy shaking the box. Blowing her messy curls out of her face, she sits back on her hands and chews on her lip like she always does when she's trying to figure out something.

"Chelly, I have something to tell you. You *can't* tell our moms. *Or* Matteo."

Now I'm worried. I sigh and look up at the ceiling. "What did you do? Ow!" My shin stings where she kicked it.

"I didn't do anything. This is serious."

I study my twin's face, and I don't think I've ever seen her look so serious. Chiara is a few minutes older, but I always feel like the big sister.

I sometimes wish I were more like her. It seems like nothing ever bothers her, but now I'm worried.

Lowering her voice, Chiara leans in toward me until I can see the little specs of green that float around in her blue eyes and the light freckles on her nose. "I think I figured out what is going on with our scars. Don't ask how I know, I just do. Twintuition or something." She rests her hand over her scar and takes a deep breath. "I can feel your heartbeat."

I sit up straighter. "What? What do you mean?"

"I mean, I think we can feel each other's hearts. Just be quiet for a sec. Empty your brain and just listen to your heart." Her eyes drift closed, and she looks peaceful for a change.

I don't know what else to do, so I follow my sister's lead and copy her. I don't really *know* how to empty my brain. I feel like I'm always thinking about something. Or worrying about something. But for my sister, I'll try my best.

If she says she can feel my heartbeat, I believe her. Chiara has a big imagination, but she wouldn't lie about something like this.

Trying to ignore all of the thoughts that usually fly around my head, I do yoga breaths like Momma taught me to help me when I get nervous. I stop thinking about all the things that make it hard for me to fall asleep, mainly getting bullied for having two moms. The bullying doesn't bother me *too* much, but I wish I could protect Kiki from it. I know Matteo is our dad, but our moms haven't told us yet. Chiara is having a hard time in school because her mind is always running in fifteen directions. Not having a lot of friends… really *any* friends, is hard for both of us. I can't stop feeling other people's feelings, and it makes me sad all the time.

I let it all fade and just feel my heart beating against my hand. The only thing I hear is Chiara breathing. Everything *feels* normal. My heart beats steadily, maybe a little fast because I'm feeling anxious. Taking another deep breath, I settle down into the carpet and think only about the tempo thumping against my chest.

And there it is. I feel it. It's so closely in sync with my own heart that I almost miss it, but it's there. *She's* there. I sob and giggle at the same time. I can feel my sister's heart! My eyes fly open. I need to see her. She's looking at me with a giant grin on her face, bathed in a golden light.

But so am I.

Kiki lets out an excited screech and throws herself at me, knocking me onto my back. "You can feel it!"

She's shaking me like a rag doll, and I yelp as she has me flailing. "Kiki! Stop! You're gonna rattle my brain loose!" But I can't stop laughing as she lets go of me and rolls over onto her back. Her hand slips into mine, and I look over at her. She looks like an angel with her own spotlight. I don't understand what this light is, but it *has* to be magic.

"What's going on? Are you okay?" Mommy and Momma fling our door open and halt in the doorway when they see us lying on the floor with the giggles. Mommy looks like she's ready to have a heart attack. Momma is all smiles, though.

"They're fine, Holly. Just being teenagers. Ugh, *teenagers.* Come downstairs and get your gifts from your uncles and put them away. You can watch TV for half an hour, then it's bedtime."

"Okay, Momma!" we say together and laugh even more.

"Help me make them a snack, love. They're fine."

I sit up and look at Mommy. She looks so scared, like she doesn't believe we're fine. "I'm sorry we scared you, Mommy. We're okay. Just goofing around."

She wipes at her eye and puts on what I know is her brave face. "Just gave me a little scare. Get your pj's on and come downstairs." She lingers for another second, then softly closes our door.

"Is she okay?" Chiara sounds genuinely concerned. "Oh. The scar thing. Yeah, I don't think we can tell her it's because we can feel each other's hearts. That's insane. But I don't want to go to the doctor either. I have art in the morning. It's the only class I like, and I don't want to miss it."

I don't want to go to the doctor either, but I also don't want Mommy to be so upset. I can feel her worry and sadness filling my chest, and it makes me want to cry. It's heavy and pushes down on me like it will crush me.

"I'll see if I can convince Momma not to call the doctor. I think she can calm her down." I *hope* she can calm her down. Her worrying makes it hard to breathe.

I spend the rest of the night lying wide awake, feeling every bit of my mom's stress. Kiki is snoring away in her bed. I put all of my focus into finding her heartbeat alongside my own. When I find it, beating steadily in time, I finally sleep.

SCENE NINE

PITTSBURGH

I HAD TO STAY after school today for a Science Club meeting. Kiki went home, and ever since she left, it has felt like there is a hole in my heart. I don't understand it. It's not natural. I tried researching during study hall today, but I didn't find an explanation.

Chiara always talks about our "twintuition," that we always know what the other is thinking, but this feels different. It's not just like finishing each other's sentences or knowing when the other person is sad, even if they aren't acting sad. This is physical.

And it hurts.

Mommy picks me up, and I try to act like everything is normal. It takes a lot of strength *not* to rub at my scar. It will just scare her, and I'll end up at the emergency room after I convinced her this morning that we don't need a doctor.

The closer we get to home, though, the less tightness I feel. As soon as we walk in the door, there is instant relief. The feeling in my chest disappears, and I'm whole again. The spot where my sister lives is beating at full strength.

Chiara is sitting at the kitchen table with Momma doing homework. I want to run to her and hug her, but I keep it cool and drop my backpack on the floor and sit down, stealing a handful of popcorn from the bowl next to her math book.

I think she must feel the same, because I've never seen her happy about a math problem, but she is grinning at the paper in front of her.

"Hi, Keeks."

"Get your own popcorn, Chelly." Her smile melts into a scowl as I shovel a second handful into my mouth. Slowly, I reach for another and start placing pieces one at a time into my mouth. My fingers find a *Peanut M&M*, so now I know why she doesn't want to share. I quickly swipe another *M&M* from the bowl and run upstairs, hearing her chair tip over as she chases after me.

"Girls! Be careful!" Mommy yells after us, but I'm already in our room, laughing hysterically while I lean on the door, trying to keep her from getting in.

"Marcella! Ugh! You're being such a jerk!" She keeps pushing her shoulder into the door, and then I'm flying down to the floor as she gets a good shove in. "Shit. I'm sorry, Chelly!"

Chiara helps me up. My elbow is scraped with carpet burn and stings.

I hear footsteps running down the hall, and Momma bursts into the room with smoke practically coming out of her ears. "Girls! You have *got* to calm down! Fifteen minutes of quiet time."

I hate when our moms have to yell at us. They hardly ever do, so it sucks when they feel like they have to. "We're sorry, Momma. We'll stop," I tell her, and she sighs and shakes her head.

"You two remind me so much of your Aunt Tracy and me. I know it's normal for siblings to fight, but please be more careful, so one of you doesn't get hurt." She lowers her voice. "You know Mommy is a little nervous about things right now. Please. For her, take it easy."

I feel a twinge in my chest as both my sister's and my hearts sink. "I'm sorry." Chiara gets up and hugs our mom. Momma kisses her forehead, but I notice she has to stand on her toes slightly. Momma is petite, and Chiara passed her up in height this year. She still isn't as tall as I am, though.

"I know, sweetie. You're good kids. Wouldn't trade either of you for the world." She lets go of my sister and beckons me to her. "Your turn.

Hugs." I jump up and hug her as tightly as I can.

Momma reminds us of our mandatory "calm down" time and quietly shuts our door. I flop down on my bed and pick up the book from my night table. Aunt Tracy bought me *The Hunger Games* books for my birthday, and I stayed up late last night reading under my covers with my book light so I wouldn't wake up Kiki, but it's so good I couldn't stop reading.

Chiara is sitting cross-legged on her bed with her box from the antique store, slowly turning it this way and that, trying to figure out how she's going to open it. Every time she turns it, the contents thump against the lid. I can't stand watching her struggle, so I close my book and look through the drawer on my desk for something to help her pry it open. I find a metal bookmark. That may work.

"Here. Gimme." I sit at the bottom of her bed and hold out my hand.

Frustrated, she hands it over and falls backward to lie down, shaking the bed. "Good luck. Nothing ever works."

The lock itself is really old and rusty. I think if I jam the bookmark into the seam of the box, the lock may just pop open. I try a few times, but nothing happens, other than my bookmark bending. I huff and try again with the same result.

Chiara is lying on her back, playing on her phone. "Told you," she tells me, sounding bored.

I'm determined. I'm getting this box open for her. I yank on the lock as hard as I can and almost fall off the bed when it breaks off. "You did it!" Chiara yells, slapping her hands over her mouth. She cringes, knowing we're supposed to be having quiet time. "You did it!" she whisper yells.

The box feels warm in my hands, and a sense of calm settles over me, which is odd. It's... serene. I hand my sister her treasure, excited to see what is inside.

"It would be so cool if it's full of money." She removes the broken piece of the lock and lifts the lid. The hinges squeak from years of being stuck closed. Chiara's face lights up.

"What? Is it money?" I slide across the bed to sit next to her and eagerly peer into the box.

"It's… weird cards. Look how cool they are!" She hands me the deck of cards, each with different photos and labels, and goes back to pulling out items. "A really old notebook. Oh! Another notebook." Stuff starts falling out from between the pages when she lifts out the second leather-bound journal. Old photographs, letters, and train tickets scatter across her violet and turquoise quilt.

I abandon the deck of cards and pick through pictures with my sister, handling them gently, afraid I will tear them. Chiara is sorting things into piles- photos, letters, and other items. I pick up a photo that is yellowed around the edges and slightly brittle. It's of two women, maybe in their twenties or thirties? They're in a garden, sitting on a bench.

The weird pulsing in my chest from yesterday at the pizza shop is back. I rub at the scar, trying to force it to stop. I narrow my eyes and look more closely at the photo. There is something familiar about the women. One is curvy with brown hair that is curled, with half of it pinned up. The other is willowy, and I think blonde, but she has a cap on her head.

Chiara is also studying a photo, brows furrowed and biting on the side of her lip. "Do you…" she starts, then exhales through her nose and picks up a different photo. "Uh… Chelly." I feel Chiara's heart thundering in my own chest right alongside my own as I think we're both coming to the same conclusion.

Photo after photo, we pass them back and forth, making sure we're seeing the same thing. Finally, our eyes meet. Her blue eyes are wide and practically glittering. The gold light is back, outlining her like her own personal sunbeam.

"This isn't possible, right?" she mutters. "Like… this is crazy. Right, Chelly?"

I don't know what to say. I keep staring at the photo in my hands of the two women on horseback, laughing. Chiara has moved on to the other items, opening a journal to the middle. After scanning a few lines, the color drains from her face, and the journal drops from her hands like it burned her, landing face down.

"Kiki! Be careful you don't rip the pages!" I pick it up, smoothing the pages and making sure they aren't torn when my eyes land on the words that made my sister drop the book. The handwriting is swirly, just like Chiara's.

June 25, 1887

Marcella is finally here. After almost one hundred years, my sister has come back to me. Mr. McGreavy gave her the apartment across the hall from me, but we have spent our nights together, sleeping in either my apartment or hers. The pull in my chest is finally at ease having her near.

My hands shake as I turn the page and the next and the next. Page after page, Chiara writes about her life with Marcella over one hundred years ago. I scan as quickly as my eyes will allow me, trying to absorb whatever this is.

Chiara is next to me, hugging her knees to her chest and staring into space. I know her, though, and she is trying to figure this out, but her brain isn't caught up yet. I pick up the other journal and take a breath before opening it to a random page. This one is a dream journal.

As I read the first entry, everything goes fuzzy, and my head feels light. The words are distorted and swimming around the page in swirls. Suddenly, my body seizes and images flash across my vision like a movie playing on fast forward.

It's an intense montage of two women in different time periods. Sometimes they look like they are having so much fun together, but there are also intense moments of pain and scenes that look like a horror movie. Fire, and blood, and violence. They always look like Chiara and I. But through it all, I feel love so overwhelming I could burst open and have it come spilling out of me like a rainstorm.

When it ends, I collapse on the bed, and everything goes dark.

SCENE TEN

PITTSBURGH

"GIRLS! DINNER IS READY!"

"Mmmm." I groan and crack an eye open. My vision is blurry, and I feel like I got hit by a truck. Mommy is calling us from down the hall.

"We'll be right there!" Hands jostle me. "Chelly! Wake up!" Chiara hisses.

Squinting against the sunlight shining through our window, I pull myself up to sit and rub my eyes. "What happened?"

"We passed out. Help me clean this up!" My sister is frantically shoving everything back into the box. I neatly gather up the pile of letters and train tickets and tuck them into one of the journals while she stacks the photos so they fit, then tucks the box under her pillow.

We just stare at each other, unsure of what to say, but knowing we have a hard conversation ahead. She's absently playing with the cornicello charm on her necklace. Uncle Teo's mom gave them to us for our tenth birthdays. She always does that when she's nervous. I take her hand in mine and nod, letting her know we're okay, and we head downstairs to dinner.

The only thing I do know is that our lives just changed forever.

We rush through dinner and race back to our room after we help clean the dishes. I think our moms are suspicious that we're up to something, but I don't care. Chiara and I need to talk— right now.

We're seated on the floor with the box between us, and I don't even know how to begin this conversation, but I don't need to, because Kiki is already there.

She's squeezing my hands so hard she may crush my bones. "Marcella! We did it! We finally did it!" Her eyes plead with me to understand what she is saying. And I do.

There is a fire blazing behind my star, but it's different than the flames that consumed me over four hundred years ago. It's… exciting.

The universe finally heard our prayer. Chiara is my sister, not my friend, whom I love as my sister, but my honest and true sister from the moment we were born.

But then again, maybe we always were. Maybe it just took our will and our magic to bring us here today so that we could be the people we were always meant to be.

Chiara's cheeks are wet with happy tears. My throat hurts from the giant lump forming. I choke out a sob, and I'm suddenly wrapped in my sister's arms. Her fingers dig into my skin, and her wild hair is in my mouth, but I don't care. I hug her back just as fiercely, crying into her shoulder.

The spell she cast to bind our souls finally achieved something that shouldn't be possible. We beat every force that tried to keep us apart.

I don't know how, but I hug her even harder, afraid that if I let go, this somehow won't be true. It will just be a dream. "Ti amo, sorella mia. Ti amo così tanto."

At that, the tears stop. We slowly pull away from each other in stunned silence. "Did I just…" No. That can't be right. Can it?

Chiara throws her arms in the air in triumph. "Holy shit, Chelly!"

"Language!"

She ignores me. "We speak Italian! Wait… WAIT. Whoa. *Whoooa.*" She clears her throat and flips her hair over her shoulder, giving me a smoldering look. "Nous sommes des sorcières." She waggles her eyebrows, and I burst out laughing. *We are witches.*

"Wow. We speak Italian and French?" Something else tickles my brain. "Uh, I think I speak Gaelic, too."

"*I speak Gaelic*," Chiara says in a mocking tone as she digs through the box. "Show off." Flipping through the stack of photos, she pauses on one, studying it. "Chelly, do you know what this means?"

Tilting my head, I give her a questioning look. "That we used magic to become sisters? Yeah, I know that."

She holds up a photo next to her head. "No. It means I'm never going to cry over some lame guy named Kyle in high school. Look at me! I'm gonna be a smoke show!"

I roll my eyes.

"Don't be like that. Look! You are, too!" She thrusts a photo at me. It's presumably me in a flowy, floral skirt with a blouse tucked into it, sitting on the edge of a water fountain. I'm seated with my legs up, knees bent, and my arms are raised above my head. My hair falls down my back in gentle waves. It also appears I'm never going to escape being curvy. Since I got my period a few months ago, it seems like my hips have decided to absolutely take over my body.

Chiara takes my face in between her hands and forces me to look at her. "You're beautiful, Marcella. In every life, you are the most beautiful person I know." She lifts my chin up. "There. Own it."

I nod around the tightness in my throat, but I keep my head up.

Because now I know I am powerful. *We* are powerful.

SCENE ELEVEN

PITTSBURGH

I CAN'T SLEEP. EVERY night, the memories of my past lives come in waves, and honestly, it's made me afraid to sleep. I dream of what my life was like in Italy, in London… and the worst is Paris. Watching my sister die in my arms is the hardest. These dreams have been haunting me for weeks, ever since we opened the box that revealed our truth.

Chiara is flopping around on her bed. The same thing is happening to her.

Every night after dinner, we compare our dreams to El and Nora's journals. The journals were originally started by El— I mean Chiara— who started having visions of Marcella on our birthday. Once Marcella got her memories back, she recorded her own personal history.

"Move over." Chiara climbs into my bed, not even waiting for me to make space. She is clutching her stuffed bunny, Laurence. The name makes a lot of sense now. We always thought it was weird she named a stuffed animal Laurence, but now she and I understand. She made it at Build-a-Bear for our tenth birthday and has slept with it every night since.

I huddle next to her, Laurence between us, and pull the covers up to our chins. I already feel better, just by her being here in my space.

"Chelly?" she whispers.

"Yeah?"

"This is hard." Her voice cracks, and her pain radiates deep into my soul. Pulling her into me, her body shakes as she muffles her sobs in my pillow so our moms won't hear through the wall. I press my cheek to the top of her head and just let her cry. I don't ask her to tell me what caused it tonight.

I have my own nightmares of a man named Charles. An inquisitor.

Kat and Laurence.

Olivier.

But every night, the dreams come in relentless waves, and all we can do is be there for each other.

It's not all bad. We had so many incredible times together, especially as Nora and Elsie. It's almost like every time we were reborn, we were closer and closer to what we are now. I especially love the stories of their travels. It's inspiring— it's what I want for us.

But the hard times are especially difficult to relive.

And it's freaky to think that we've both been married before. We've done… adult things.

Those are the craziest dreams and make me uncomfortable. Neither of us talks about those memories.

Chiara eventually cries herself to sleep, but I stay up all night holding her to me, hoping that if I keep her close, she won't have another nightmare.

SCENE TWELVE

PITTSBURGH

WHEN I GET HOME from science club, I'm exhausted. I didn't sleep at all last night.

I follow the sounds of voices into the kitchen and find Chiara seated with Mommy. Her tarot cards are spread on the table, and she is pointing to one card while she describes something, her voice low and serious. Mommy is locked in, hanging on her every word.

In our free time, Chiara has been practicing the tarot deck. She's always been intuitive, though, so it's not surprising that it was easy for her to relearn. She's very spiritual and into mysticism like Mommy. It's been good for them to bond over. Mommy makes special tea, and Chiara does her reading and teaches her what the cards mean. I really think she's just relieved that my sister found something that she can put her focus into that is healthy, besides drawing, which she is amazing at!

I don't want to interrupt their time together, so I go upstairs and flop face down on my bed. I lie motionless for a few minutes, then drag myself up to sit and pull my journal from my night table.

I've been focusing more on journaling and learning the spells in one of the journals. It's called a grimoire. Momma bought me candle-making supplies, and I'm trying to imbue magic into candles using different dried flowers and herbs, like Chiara used to. Her grimoire details a lot of uses for flowers and what they mean. Momma is doing her best to get me the flowers I ask for from the florist. She thinks it's just to make them pretty or to smell good. So far, I'm not sure anything has worked, but she proudly burns them.

Chiara's first family grimoire was burned. I remember feeling her heart break the moment it was thrown into the fire in our cottage in Italy. I've been translating the one she rewrote as Elsie into Italian to surprise her. I haven't even attempted to draw the flowers and stuff, but Kiki can do that and make it pretty. It would be wrong for me to take that from her.

I lose myself in writing a new spell that I hope will help ease the pain of our nightmares, especially for Chiara.

There is nothing I wouldn't do to protect her from pain, as I always have.

SCENE THIRTEEN

PITTSBURGH

JULY 2012

OUR MOMS LEFT FOR a trip, just the two of them, for their fifteenth anniversary, so we're staying with Matteo and Uncle Rob. Chiara is out grocery shopping with Uncle Rob, so I have some time alone with our dad. I'm sitting at the table on the patio working on the grimoire when he comes out with a can of Cherry Coke for me. It's my favorite.

"What are you doing, Chells Bells?" He sets down my drink, and instinctively, I move my arm over the book so he can't see what I'm writing.

He narrows his eyes at me and crosses his arms and cocks a hip. "Chells. That isn't a Burn Book, is it?"

"Oh my gosh. No! It's just my journal." Please, *oh please,* let him drop this.

He eyes me suspiciously for a second, but smiles as he pulls out the chair next to me. "You're allowed to have your privacy, Marcella. I promise, I won't look at it. Just promise me that if something is bothering you, you'll talk to me. I'm much cooler than your moms. Especially Holly. Have I ever shown you pictures of your mom in college? The hair." He cringes and mouths the word 'wow,' making a gesture like her hair was huge. "Tragic."

I giggle and close the grimoire. "I definitely need to see those later." I sip my Coke and tap nervously on the rim. I don't feel Chiara, so I know she and Rob aren't on their way back from the store yet.

I need to do this while I have Matteo alone.

"You okay, kiddo?"

"Yeah, it's just… I have something I want to tell you, but I guess I'm a little scared."

"You can tell me anything, sweetie. But if you're not ready, it's okay. It's not something that can hurt you, is it?" He shifts his chair a little closer to mine and rests his hand on top of one of mine.

"No. I swear. I umm…" Just do it, Marcella. Rip off the band-aid. I take a deep breath, and the words come spilling out. "I know that you're my dad. *Our* dad."

His breath catches, eyes wide with panic. "Did your mom—"

"No. No, she didn't tell me anything. But like… I have eyes. I look just like you, and I feel something different with you. I'm not mad. I'm actually really happy that it's you."

His shoulders relax, and his brown eyes that look so much like my own are glassy. "Oh, Marcella. We were going to tell you girls, eventually. I'm sorry it's happening like this."

I smile. "I'm not. I'm glad I got to talk to you alone. I love you, and I'm proud to be your daughter."

I get out of my seat and sit on Matteo's lap so I can hug him. We're both crying, but it's a cleansing type of cry. Like the truth is finally out, and we can finally be ourselves. He can just be my dad, and I can be his daughter.

"I love you so much, Marcella. You and Chiara are my greatest treasure."

I'm so caught up in this moment with my dad that I don't even hear or feel Chiara and Rob come home.

"What's going on out here? Did someone die?" Chiara's voice shatters the moment.

I wipe my eyes on the back of my hand. "No! I just needed a hug."

She looks between us, eyes bouncing back and forth, and a look of realization crosses her face. "You told Teo you know he's our dad."

"You knew?" I ask, astounded. We've never spoken about this. I always assumed she didn't know.

"Duh. I have *eyes,* Chelly." She points dramatically at her eyes, opening them as wide as she can.

Our dad is sitting in stunned silence, not knowing what to do with us. Chiara fixes that and comes up behind his chair, wrapping her arms around his neck and kissing his cheek. "Love you, Dad."

"I love you more."

"It's not a contest!" she accuses.

"I am going to have so much to explain to Holly and Rachel when they get back." He sounds exasperated, but his smile may be permanently plastered to his face.

SCENE FOURTEEN

PITTSBURGH

JULY 2014

"WHATCHA DOING?" I STEP out onto the deck. Chiara is lying on a lounge chair playing on her phone, muttering to herself in Italian.

"Duolingo. Killin it, by the way," she says, not looking away from the screen.

"Uh, why are you using Duolingo? We're fluent." I lift her legs and sit at the end of the chair, resting her feet on my lap.

She huffs an exaggerated sigh. "Dude, there is no way for us to explain to the moms that we speak *several* languages. Seriously, Marcella. You need to learn to be, like, fifty percent *more* sneaky. Can't get away with anything with you around."

I tickle the bottom of her foot, and she kicks out and swings up to sit, tucking her feet under her. "You're so annoying." Chiara sticks her tongue out at me, but she's smiling.

And she's right. I pull out my phone and download the app.

"See? Now we can talk shit on our cousins at Thanksgiving right in front of their faces." Her eyebrows bounce playfully, smile full of mischief.

"That's rude." I create a login, but set the phone aside instead of playing. "Hey, I have something for you."

My sister's face perks up, her blue eyes twinkling in the soft glow of the garden lanterns hanging above us. I hand her a leather-bound book, and she looks at me skeptically. Reading isn't her strong suit. She was diagnosed with dyslexia when we turned fourteen. She's getting better with learning support services at school, but it still makes her self-conscious, so a book isn't the top of her list for gifts.

"I promise it's not Shakespeare." I give her an encouraging smile motion for her to take the book. She accepts it and opens to the first page. I wait patiently for it to click with her.

Her hand moves to cover her mouth. "Marcella. Is this… is this the Davazati grimoire?"

"Elsie recreated it in English, so I translated it into Italian for you. I also added the spells from Odette and Cat in French. Look." I slide closer to her and flip to the page where the spell that bound us in my ancestors' cottage lives. I read it to her in Italian, and I'm transported back to that moment where we stood at the table by the hearth, uttering the words that proved to us that the most important ingredient of magic is your love and your will.

Her hand slides into mine. "You're my best friend, Marcella."

I boop her nose, and it wrinkles on contact. "And you're mine."

The glass door to the deck slides open, and our moms come out to join us. Mom has a tray of snacks, and Momma has drinks.

"Momma, are those margaritas? Gimme, gimme!" Chiara makes grabby hands at the fancy glasses with umbrellas in them.

"Chiara! I'm a cool mom, but I'm not *that* cool. Non-alcoholic for you and your sister."

"Boooo." She takes her drink anyway and sips it.

The tray is piled with fruit, veggies, dip, and cheese.

I dig into the pineapple and yogurt dip. "Thanks, moms."

"You're welcome, Starlight. It's so hot out. We thought we could all use something to cool us off." Mom settles into a seat across from us and holds her drink to her forehead for a moment before drinking it. "What are you doing out here?"

"We started learning Italian on Duolingo. We're just practicing," Chiara responds quickly. "Posso avere dei biscotti?"

Mom's eyebrows raise. "Impressive. You didn't just hex me, did you?" She teases.

"She asked you for cookies," I translate, proving that I am also learning. Chiara gives me an approving look, which makes my scar pulse happily.

"How on brand of you, Star Fire. There are some *Oreos* in the cabinet."

My sister nearly trips running to the kitchen. "Kiki! Bring me the *Doritos*!"

"So much for our nice, healthy snack." Mom shakes her head. I make a show of eating another piece of pineapple and a strawberry for good measure, and she throws a grape at me. "*You* are supposed to be my easy child."

"I am." I eat the grape.

Chiara returns with the snacks, and we spend the night outside with our moms playing several heated rounds of *UNO*. I'm exhausted from the heat and a bit of a sugar crash by the time I crawl into my bed after midnight.

Just as I feel myself nodding off, my mattress dips with my sister's weight. "Kiki, I was almost asleep," I whine and kick her shin. "Go back to your bed."

She shoves me and climbs in anyway. I bury my face in my pillow and try to ignore her, accepting that she isn't going anywhere. This happens at least once a week since we were old enough to sleep in our own beds. I usually don't mind, but I really want to sleep.

"Chelly, I have an idea."

I turn my head so I can look at her with one eye, the other still buried in my pillow. "Do I even want to know?"

"Yes, you do. Get up. You can sleep tomorrow."

She's not giving up. With an exasperated sigh, I roll to my side and face her. "Well?" I press.

"I was thinking, what if we move to Italy?" She looks so proud of herself for coming up with this idea.

"We're in high school. I don't think any of our parents are going to pick up and move to Italy." I pause. "Maybe Dad. He seems like your best chance."

She flicks my forehead and hisses, "Not now. Use your brain, Marcella. When we're done with high school. And college. And art school. You know, once we're adults."

Now I'm awake. "So, hypothetically, we move to Italy. What do we do there?"

"Whatever we want! I just want to see where we're from. What might be there for us?" She opens her phone and pulls up a map of Italy, zooming in on a place in Florence. "See this? This is where we lived. Aren't you the least bit curious to see what it looks like now? What is in place of our home?"

Our home. The Pallacioni family cottage was burned with us. The memory of that horrific night takes hold, stinging my eyes.

But against all odds, my sister and I rose from the ashes. We *won*. Over and over, we have defied every person and every system that told us we weren't good enough, that we weren't deserving of our independence and our agency. Our dreams. Maybe something good rose from the ashes of our home.

We've lived five lives, and throughout those lives, the one constant was our love. My home is my sister, and it doesn't matter where in the world or in time we are. She is my home. Not a place. *Her.*

Slowly, my lips turn up. "Wherever you go, I go."

SCENE FIFTEEN

MONTEFIORALLE

MARCH 2026

I PUSH MY SUNGLASSES on top of my head, taking in the site where my family home once stood. A stunning stone villa blanketed in vines that no doubt will sprout colorful flowers in the coming weeks as spring awakens nature's greenery, stands in place of the humble cottage of my first life.

Terra cotta pots line the walkway, and two bikes are leaned against the house near the front door. While I don't recognize the house in front of me as *mine*, the energy from the building is familiar— like the remnants of the family of my past still have a place here, watching over its new inhabitants.

"It needs a goat."

"Kiki," I chastise.

"What? We had a goat. It needs a goat." She shields her eyes from the blinding, late-day sun. "One in pajamas."

I snort a laugh at my sister trying to make light of this moment that feels so heavy with grief. It's a gift to be able to see what's become of the home that taught me the true meaning of love, but it doesn't make the pain any less tolerable knowing the innocence that was stolen from us in this very spot. I still have nightmares of that night, even several lives later. But having Chiara here, knowing we can never be torn apart again, helps ease the ache.

Her arm slides across my shoulders, and she pulls me into a side hug. "Let's go check out our new place. Our moms and Dad are waiting."

I give our old home one last wistful glance and head back in the direction of town. Our parents are staying with us for the first month to help us get settled into our new life in Montefioralle. Unfortunately, Rob wasn't able to come, but he promised to visit next time our dad comes later this year with our grandma. I don't want to think about how much I'll miss him. He is just as much our dad as Matteo.

I think part of the magic that bound us together worked in other ways. I don't think about my life as Audrey, only the time Chiara and I spent in France after she saved me from the hell I was living. We were granted great loves in Olivier and Laurence, and I am grateful to carry a piece of Olivier with me. But, as Nora and El, we gained a greater gift. We were able to truly find ourselves as we never had before.

And now, we are back where it all started with a new family. While our families never replace the ones we left behind, this one is different. Our magic gave us the last missing piece of our lives: a family that chooses each other over all else.

We found a retail space for rent that has a spacious apartment upstairs. Our parents helped us secure the funding we needed to start up our business. In honor of the apothecary and parfumerie of our past lives, we are opening our own spell shop. We specialize in candles, teas, stationery and art prints designed by Chiara, and bath and body products made from sustainable materials. All of our products are imbued with intention, thanks to the grimoire.

We wind our way through town, taking our time and soaking in the rhythm and energy. It feels peaceful, unhurried. It's the perfect place for us to start the next chapter of our lives.

Our parents are standing outside the building, guarding the boxes of our belongings that we had shipped over. We didn't bring too much. Mostly our clothes and trinkets that are important to us. We can buy everything else we need here.

"There you are! Where did you go off to?" Momma asks.

"Just exploring the neighborhood a bit." I hug her, then Mom, who is on the verge of crying. Again. "Mom, you're cutting off my air supply."

"Hey, mommy dearest, let go of the girl. I'm not dressed to be on the news after that flight." My dad pulls Mom off of me and holds her to him because she's now fully sobbing.

Chiara claps her hands to get everyone's attention. "Okay, as great as it is making a scene in the middle of this gorgeous Italian town, can we please move it inside and start unpacking?"

I can't wait to see our apartment in person. The moving company moved our furniture a few days ago, so we should be good to stay here tonight. Our parents are staying down the road in an Airbnb.

My hand is shaking as I try to put the key in the lock, fumbling it twice before the lock clicks open. Taking a cleansing breath, I push open the door and enter the shop space. "Oh wow." It's even more beautiful in person.

Chiara pushes through everyone. "Let me see! Holy shit." She jumps on me and starts shaking me. "Chelly, we did it! This is *ours*!"

I don't even try to remain calm, and start jumping and shrieking with her like we did when we were kids. We stop and turn to our parents, who are standing in the doorway, grinning like crazy at us.

"Why are you just standing there? We're celebrating!" Chiara grabs Dad's hands and starts swinging in circles with him.

I hold my hands out to our moms. "Well?" They crush me in a mom sandwich, laughing and crying.

This is officially the best day of any of my many lives.

SCENE SIXTEEN

MONTEFIORALLE

"IS THAT CROOKED?" I stand back and look at the sign on our front window. *Due di Tazze Mercantili* is opening in just a few days. We named our shop after the Two of Cups tarot card. Chiara designed the logo and hand-painted our sign.

The card represents where we are now in our lives. The shop represents our connection to one another. She incorporated our star sign, Pisces, into the design. The two fish swim in infinity above the cups, and primroses lie at the base of the chalices.

My sister joins me outside and studies the sign. "No, I think it's good. Maybe it's just you that's crooked." She paints a streak of blue on my arm with her paintbrush and runs back inside before I can react.

I wish our parents could be here for opening day, but they had to go back to the States last week. Chiara and I are finding the rhythm of our lives without them, and in this place that is now our home.

Heading back inside, I grab a box of lip balms from by the door and set up the display by the cash register. I made lemon-mint scented lip balms for our grand opening. They smell divine and make your lips smooth and nourished for hours. I imbued this batch with luck.

A bunch of boxes falls over near the back door, and I nearly jump out of my skin. Chiara goes running to see what happened. "Awwww! Chelly!" She is talking in a baby voice, so I have literally no idea what is going on. I make my way around the displays in the middle of the room and into the back room, where I find my sister snuggled up with a white

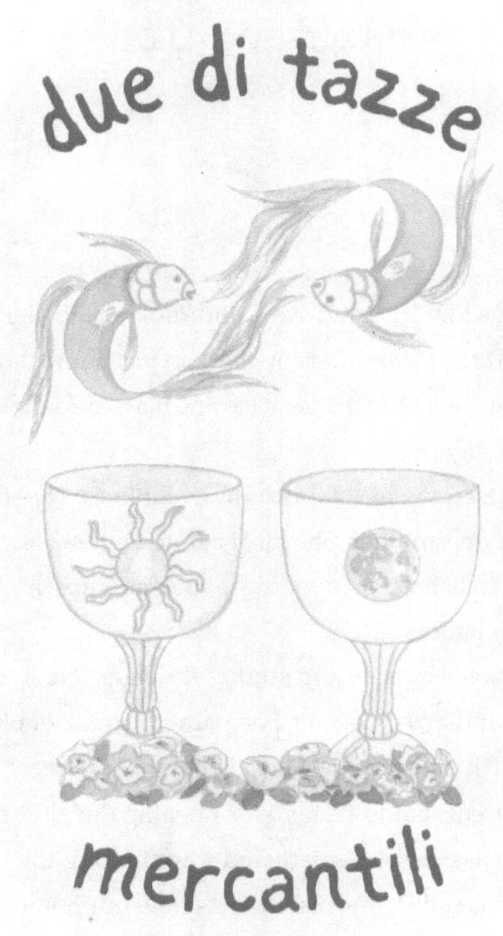

cat with black spots. It looks like a little cow.

"Baby mucca. Oh my gosh, it's so cute." She buries her face in its fur, and, to the cat's credit, it seems to be eating up the attention, making biscuits on her shoulder and purring loudly.

"It might belong to someone," I tell her. "Should we check outside to see if anyone is looking for it?"

Chiara looks downright offended at the suggestion, holding the cat even more tightly. "Excuse me, but the cat distribution system decides who gets the cats. Mucca is officially our shop kitty. Now, please go get *our* cat some cheese and a bowl of water from upstairs."

I give the cat some rubs, and it leans into my touch. "Okay, fine. We keep it, but if someone comes looking, we have to send it back to its home."

"Psssh. Take better care of your cat. Finders keepers. Huh, Mucca?"

Oh good. She's already named the cat. Mucca means cow, which is appropriate. She lifts the cat and inspects its private region. "Okay, I *think* it's a boy." She sets him down and pats her leg for him to follow her, and he obliges, trotting at her heels into the main area of the shop.

I shake my head and go to procure a bowl of water for our new friend. When I get back, he's basking in a sunbeam in the front window like he owns the place.

I finish up with the last of the store set-up while Chiara runs out to get what we need to take care of a cat. By the time she returns, everything is set up. We decorated to emulate our work table area in the Pallacioni cottage. Dried flowers and fairy lights hang around the ceiling, with candles and flowers scattered among the bottles of product and displays. We also have a small seating area by the door to serve tea and a table on the back wall where Chiara can do tarot readings. It's warm and inviting— just the way we wanted it.

And it's ours. Our imprint, our magic, is in every nook and cranny of the shop. Chiara's personal touches of art hang on the walls. My favorite is a painting of an eight-pointed star with our glowing silhouettes against a field of stars. Framed photos of El and Nora are also strewn about, honoring the women who truly made this possible for us. They were our truest inspiration.

This shop, this life, is everything I dreamed it would be and so much more.

We eat dinner that night in the shop. Mucca rubs against our legs, begging for bits of chicken, which we of course give him.

I thought I knew what it was to feel complete when Chiara and I discovered the truth of our past. I was wrong.

I don't think there is a limit on how full your heart can be. There is always room for more joy, more passion, more friendship, more life. So I will leave my heart open to whoever and whatever needs a home.

SCENE SEVENTEEN

MONTEFIORALLE

CHIARA AND I HOLD the sign on the door. "Are you ready?"

She nods, nibbling at her bottom lip. "Uno, due, tre." We flip the sign to read "Aperto," and unlock the door.

Due di Tazze is officially open for business. People trickle in throughout the day. It is the first time in hundreds of years that Chiara and I have spoken exclusively in our native language, and it rolls off our tongues like a song begging to be sung.

An elderly woman buys four sachets of tea and insists that we join her for dinner the next evening. Signora Lombardy lives alone three doors down, and she informs us that her husband passed away a few years ago. We gratefully accept her invitation, and I send her home with a free sample of face cream and a lip balm.

Within a couple of hours, we sell out of lavender goat milk soap and half of the floral candles. I am dead on my feet by the time it is near closing time. We close at five, but begin cleaning up at four-thirty, when the bell tinkles on the door, announcing another customer. I look up from the table I am restocking with body cream to greet the young woman who just walked in. She looks to be about our age. Her long hair has hot pink streaks in the front, and I'm jealous of her eclectic style. She's wearing a floral maxi skirt, a cropped sweater, and pink boots. Her hair is pushed back with a headband.

Something pulls me to her, like I am supposed to know her. Or maybe I do know her? Chiara catches my eye and is silently sending me a message.

I feel a twinge in my star and rub at it, noticing Chiara is doing the same.

"Buonasera," I greet the woman.

"Buonasera." Her smile is nearly blinding. She turns to look at a display, slowly browsing the remaining stock.

Chiara drags me into the back room. "So, you feel that, right?"

I stand on my tiptoes and look over her shoulder. The girl is kneeling and petting Mucca, who is eating up the attention he has attracted all day. "Do we know her?"

She chews on her lower lip in thought. "No, but I think we're supposed to. Like now. She came into our lives now for a reason."

Her aura is pink, like Chiara's usually is when it isn't joined with my own. I see the yearning in my sister's face, but it's not romantic. It's something else.

We've never really had friends other than each other in this life. Certainly never best friends, the kind you can bear your soul to. Friends who lift you when you fall and share in the joy of your successes.

I flick my head toward the front room. "Come on. Let's go meet our new friend." I squeeze her hand in reassurance. I want this for us, especially for Chiara. She took the merciless teasing at school much harder than I did and eventually just gave up on friends. I had at least made friends in college, but my sister shied away from her classmates at art school.

Her hand is shaking, but she nods and follows me. Some scars are more difficult to heal.

"I'm Marcella. This is my sister, Chiara. And that," I point to the cat flopped over on his back accepting belly rubs, "is Mucca."

"He is a precious baby! I'm Celestina." She rises to stand, brushing off her skirt. "I just moved to town a few weeks ago from San Gimignano."

Chiara finally finds her voice. "We just moved here from the United States."

Her eyebrows nearly hit her hairline. "Your Italian is *very* good! I would have never known!"

I smile to myself. "Our family is originally from the area. What brings you here?"

"Oh." She hugs herself and looks a little uncertain. "I just needed a change."

"Us too," Chiara says, not pushing her for any further information. Celestina's posture relaxes. "Would you like to have dinner with us tonight? Our neighbor, Signora Lombardy, insists we have dinner with her every Monday. We are hosting tonight."

Celestina tugs at her sweater sleeves and shifts from foot to foot. "Are you sure? I don't want to impose."

"No imposition. We'd love to have you." I smile encouragingly, hoping I don't look overeager or like a madwoman.

She smiles sweetly. "Yes. I'd love to!"

And with that, my heart expands to make room for Celestina.

SCENE EIGHTEEN

MONTEFIORALLE

"SERIOUSLY, KIKI? WE ARE adults."

"Shush. Move over." Laurence the bunny smacks me in the face as my sister shoves her way into my bed. He's a little worse for wear after almost twenty years.

"You are ridiculous. Oof!" Mucca jumps right on my stomach, knocking the wind from me, and promptly lies down and goes to sleep on my chest.

"Are you done being dramatic?"

I wheeze, sucking in a breath. "No."

Chiara props her head up on her elbow, and I know that look in her eyes. She is about to propose something. "Out with it."

"So, we're in our fifth life together. But this time we are actually sisters. I mean, you were always my sister, but now you are my *actual* sister."

"Yes, Kiki. I know. You've been kicking me since we shared a womb. Ow!" Her foot collides with my shin. "What is actually wrong with you?"

Her face is illuminated by the moonlight shining through my bedroom window. She looks angelic, even though right now I'm certain she may be a demon. "We don't have time to get into that. So, back to the topic at hand." She sits up and turns on the lamp on my side table.

I slap my hands over my eyes. "Kiki! Retinas!"

She sighs and drags me up to sit. "This is serious, Marcella." Her clear blue eyes are hazy with grey and worry. Her heart beat is off, anxious and erratic.

"What's wrong?"

"Well, the spell finally worked the way we intended. We are sisters now, so…" she trails off.

Oh. Oh! "You think the spell is complete." She nods slowly.

"Yeah. What if this is it?" A single tear slides down her cheek, and she takes a shuddering breath. "What if this is the last life we get together?"

I had not considered that possibility. I've been so absorbed in the fact that the spell worked that it never crossed my mind that this could be the end of the line for us.

Is that what I want? Eventually, one of us is going to leave this world, leaving the other behind again. Can my heart bear that loss again, not knowing if I will ever see my sister again? Or can I end this life happy and content in the knowledge that I was blessed with five lives with my soulmate?

Is it selfish to want more? More time. More lives. More adventure.

Why shouldn't we be selfish? Love is supposed to be without limit, and my love for my sister has no end. So, no. This life isn't enough. Not when it comes to her.

I reach over and wipe her tears. "Well, what are you waiting for, cara mia?"

She cocks her head, waiting for me to elaborate, but I wait for her to get there on her own. My heart leaps in time with hers when she realizes what I am saying.

She leaps from my bed, dragging the blankets with her. "Get the grimoire, Marcella. We have work to do."

Acknowledgments

This book was a personal journey that helped heal some old wounds that have never completely closed.

This book would not be possible without Laura Cannella. We came up with the idea for the book together, and as with Marcella and Chiara, it bonded us in a uniquely beautiful way. This story belongs to both of us, as we are both represented in our characters. Thank you, Laura, for adding your creativity, heart, and passion to the art, plot, and Chiara. Thank you for the voice notes, hundreds of texts, coffee dates, and emotional support that it took to put the darker parts of myself as I found my way to the light on paper.

To Stacy and Jen: my soul sisters from the start. You have been by my side through everything, and it's your love that is reflected in the pages of this book. Friendship is powerful, and the love I feel for you both inspired so many moments of this story. The strength you've given me is poured into these characters. You're my ride or dies in every life.

Dawn, you thought you'd escape my friendship, but the joke is on you. You never stood a chance against Laura and me. Thank you for the writing dates, voice notes, texts, and encouragement throughout this process. I cannot wait to see what you do next, Dawn Darla.

To the Kickstarter backers: Thank you for believing in this book and believing in me. You made this possible, and I am forever grateful to you for your generosity.

And to my incredible team that makes this all possible: Twisted Thorns Editing, Sagen Raven Art, Feelin' Stabby Art, Umber Chocolates, EmTree Bath & Body, my Street Team, and Blue Eyed Muse Art (yes, Laura, I'm going to thank you a million times). Your support and enthusiasm for my stories and my characters make every frustrating moment, every tear, every minute where I question if I can really do this, worth the struggle. You give me the strength to keep chasing this dream. Thank you for being a part of the journey.

About the Author

Stevie Hosler writes character-driven fantasy that gets your heart racing with nonstop action, characters who feel like your best friends, and plot twists that will leave you weak in the knees. Her debut novel, paranormal fantasy *Shadow of Lilith*, was released in 2025.

Stevie lives in Pittsburgh with her husband, son, and four cats. In her free time, she runs a chapter of Silent Book Club with *The Stars in Our Hearts* artist, Laura, reads, attends a book club at her local comic store, Pittsburgh Comics, attends emo and punk concerts (It's not just a phase!), and plays on her Switch.

FOLLOW THE AUTHOR

www.ingramcontent.com/pod-product-compliance
Lightning Source LLC
LaVergne TN
LVHW091154150826
845672LV00005B/1146

9798234007537